RELIC OF THE DRAGON

IDW

Become our fan on Facebook **facebook.com/idwpublishing**
Follow us on Twitter **@idwpublishing**
Subscribe to us on YouTube **youtube.com/idwpublishing**
See what's new on Tumblr **tumblr.idwpublishing.com**
Check us out on Instagram **instagram.com/idwpublishing**

ISBN: 978-1-68405-215-8   21 20 19 18   1 2 3 4

COVER BY
MIGUEL ÁNGEL GARCÍA

TRANSLATION BY
ANNA ROSENWONG

LETTERED BY
RON ESTEVEZ

EDITED BY
JUSTIN EISINGER
AND ALONZO SIMON

PRODUCTION BY
RON ESTEVEZ

PUBLISHER
TED ADAMS

For international rights, contact licensing@idwpublishing.com

Ted Adams, CEO & Publisher
Greg Goldstein, President & COO
Robbie Robbins, EVP/Sr. Graphic Artist
Chris Ryall, Chief Creative Officer
David Hedgecock, Editor-in-Chief
Laurie Windrow, Sr. VP of Sales & Marketing
Matthew Ruzicka, CPA, Chief Financial Officer
Lorelei Bunjes, VP of Digital Services
Jerry Bennington, VP of New Product Development

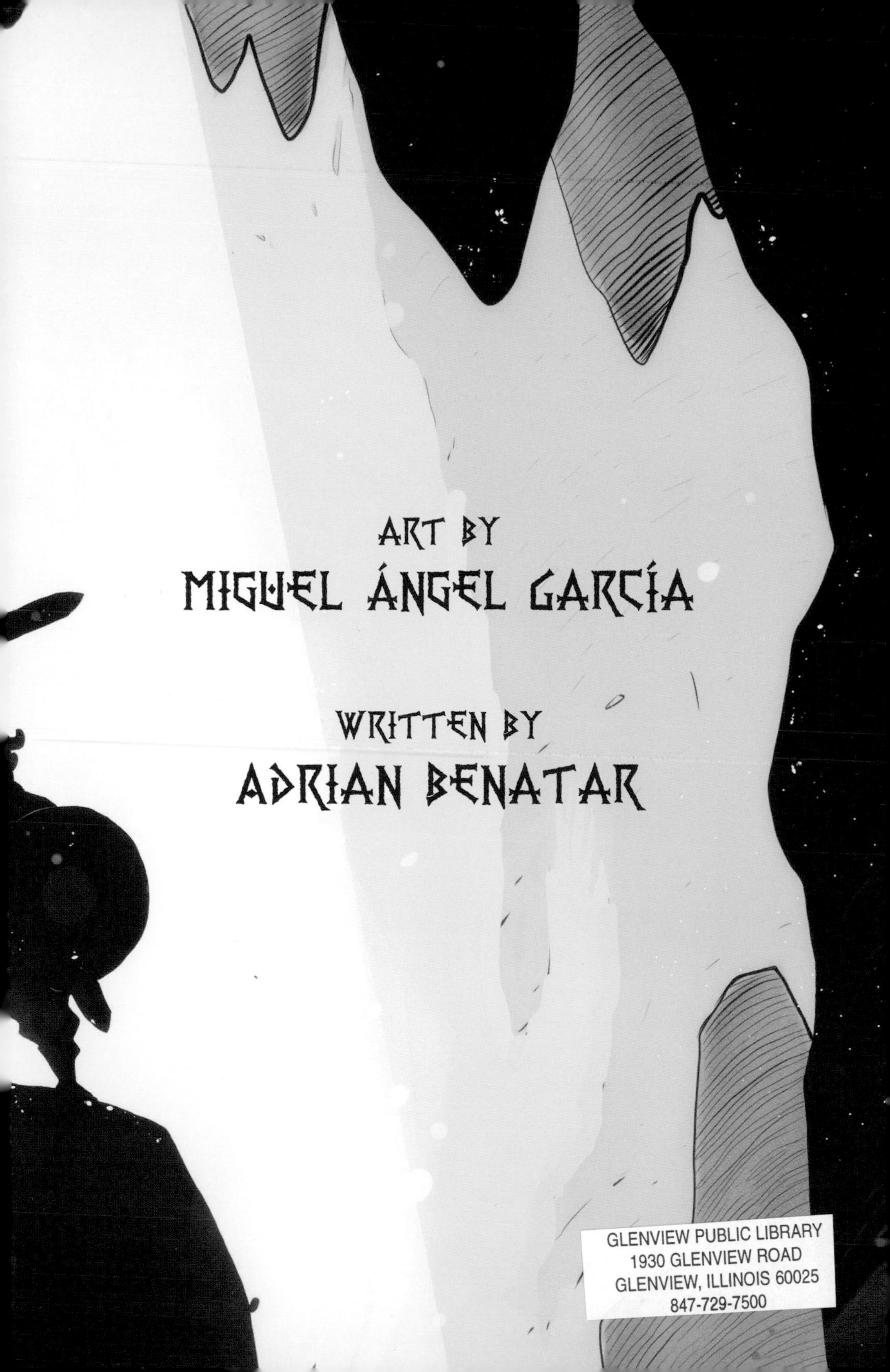

ART BY
MIGUEL ÁNGEL GARCÍA

WRITTEN BY
ADRIAN BENATAR

INTRODUCTION

WELCOME!

ARE YOU HUNGRY FOR ADVENTURE? READY TO
UNCOVER HIDDEN TREASURE, MEET FRIENDLY
STRANGERS, AND CHALLENGE THE UNKNOWN?!

THEN YOU'RE IN THE RIGHT PLACE!

YOU'VE ENTERED A WORLD WHERE THE CLEAR PATH
MAY LEAD TO A SMILING CREATURE READY
TO DEVOUR YOU IN ONE BITE!

SO BE WARNED -- NOT ALL ROUTES ARE SAFE.
YOU MUST STAY ON GUARD TO AVOID TRAPS
AND MISCREANTS.

WHEN FACED WITH A DECISION YOU WILL SEE THESE
SYMBOLS -- STAR OR SPIRAL -- THEN CHOOSE YOUR
PATH. FATE, A DICE ROLL, OR A GUIDING WORD OF
ADVICE FROM A FELLOW PLAYER MAY HELP YOU
SUCCEED IN RETURNING URIK HOME SAFE AND SOUND.

MAY THE GODS HELP YOU!

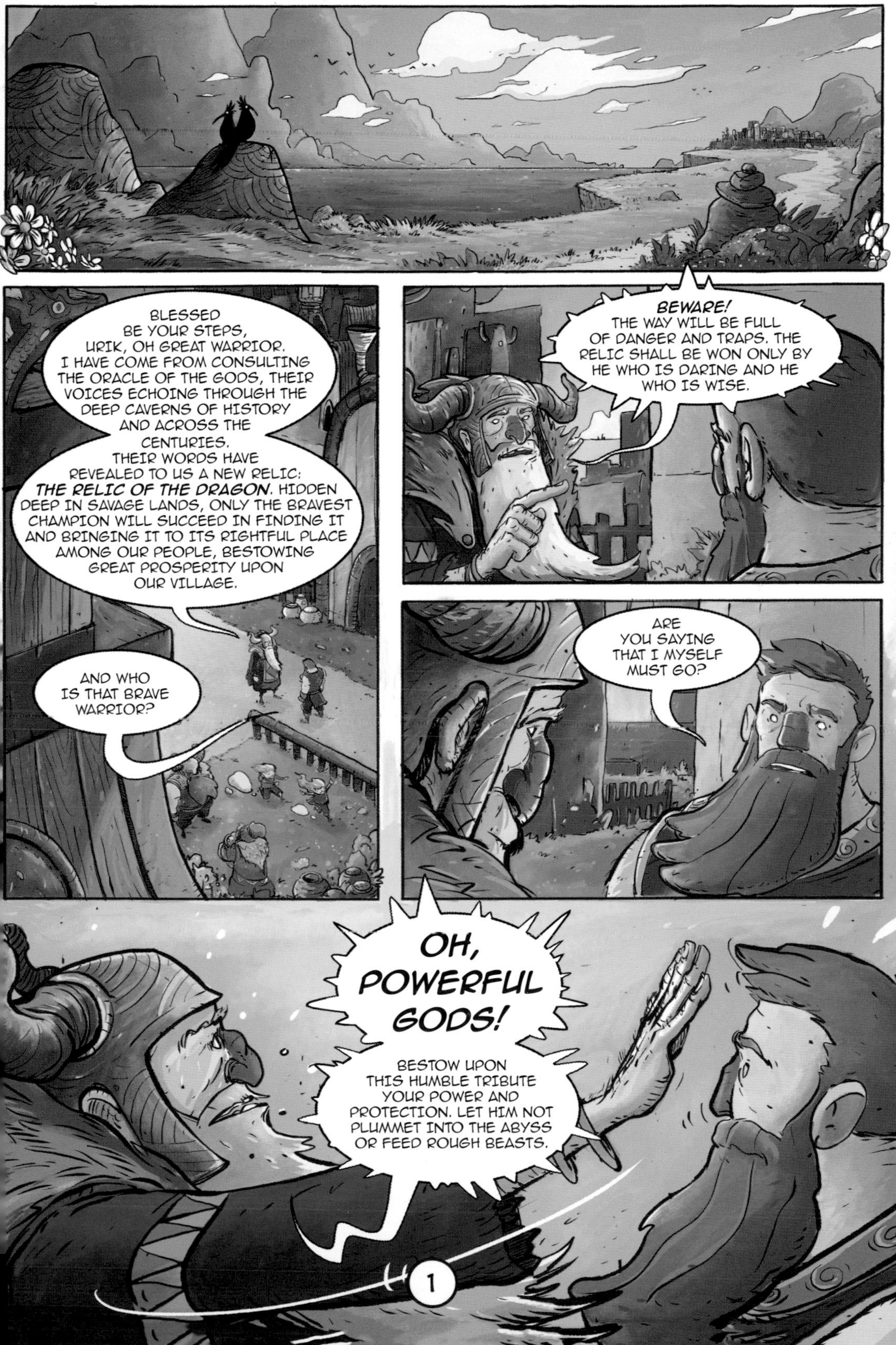
BLESSED BE YOUR STEPS, URIK, OH GREAT WARRIOR. I HAVE COME FROM CONSULTING THE ORACLE OF THE GODS, THEIR VOICES ECHOING THROUGH THE DEEP CAVERNS OF HISTORY AND ACROSS THE CENTURIES.
THEIR WORDS HAVE REVEALED TO US A NEW RELIC: *THE RELIC OF THE DRAGON*. HIDDEN DEEP IN SAVAGE LANDS, ONLY THE BRAVEST CHAMPION WILL SUCCEED IN FINDING IT AND BRINGING IT TO ITS RIGHTFUL PLACE AMONG OUR PEOPLE, BESTOWING GREAT PROSPERITY UPON OUR VILLAGE.
AND WHO IS THAT BRAVE WARRIOR?
BEWARE! THE WAY WILL BE FULL OF DANGER AND TRAPS. THE RELIC SHALL BE WON ONLY BY HE WHO IS DARING AND HE WHO IS WISE.
ARE YOU SAYING THAT I MYSELF MUST GO?
OH, POWERFUL GODS!
BESTOW UPON THIS HUMBLE TRIBUTE YOUR POWER AND PROTECTION. LET HIM NOT PLUMMET INTO THE ABYSS OR FEED ROUGH BEASTS.

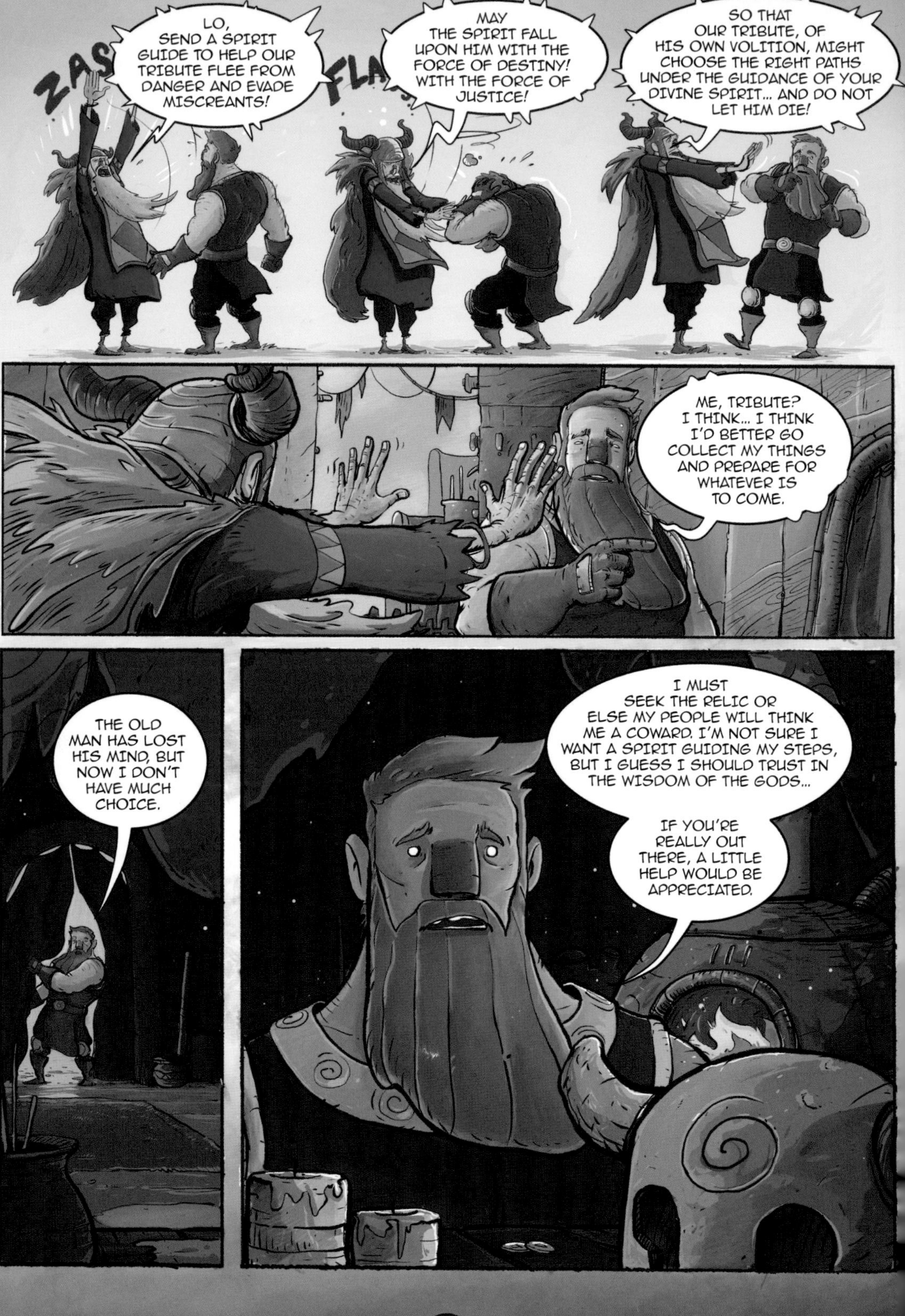
ZAS
LO, SEND A SPIRIT GUIDE TO HELP OUR TRIBUTE FLEE FROM DANGER AND EVADE MISCREANTS!
FLA
MAY THE SPIRIT FALL UPON HIM WITH THE FORCE OF DESTINY! WITH THE FORCE OF JUSTICE!
SO THAT OUR TRIBUTE, OF HIS OWN VOLITION, MIGHT CHOOSE THE RIGHT PATHS UNDER THE GUIDANCE OF YOUR DIVINE SPIRIT... AND DO NOT LET HIM DIE!
ME, TRIBUTE? I THINK... I THINK I'D BETTER GO COLLECT MY THINGS AND PREPARE FOR WHATEVER IS TO COME.
THE OLD MAN HAS LOST HIS MIND, BUT NOW I DON'T HAVE MUCH CHOICE.
I MUST SEEK THE RELIC OR ELSE MY PEOPLE WILL THINK ME A COWARD. I'M NOT SURE I WANT A SPIRIT GUIDING MY STEPS, BUT I GUESS I SHOULD TRUST IN THE WISDOM OF THE GODS...
IF YOU'RE REALLY OUT THERE, A LITTLE HELP WOULD BE APPRECIATED.

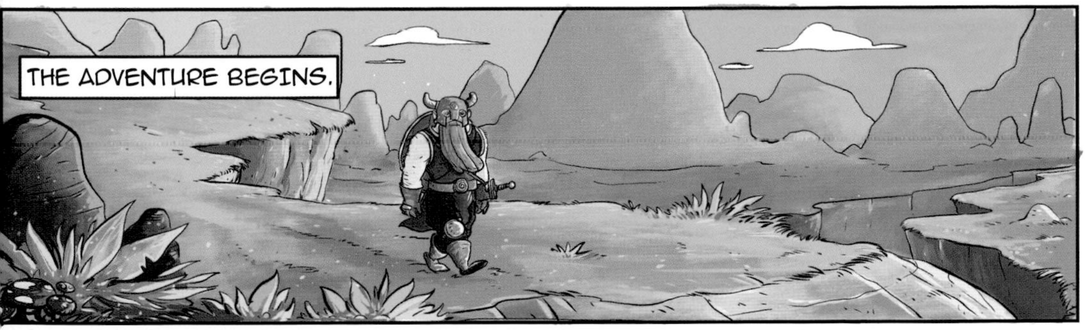
THE ADVENTURE BEGINS.

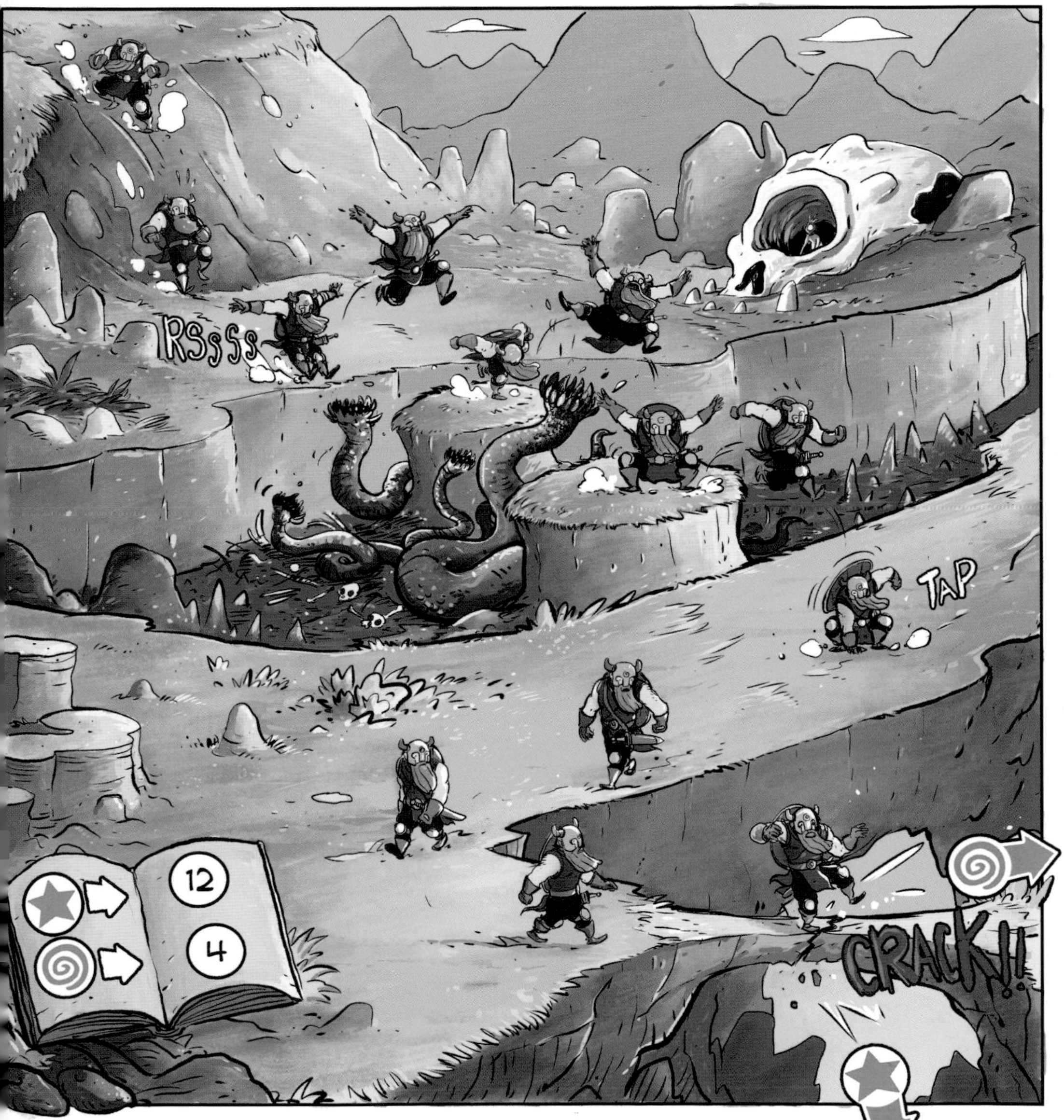
RSsSS
TAP
12
4
CRACK!!

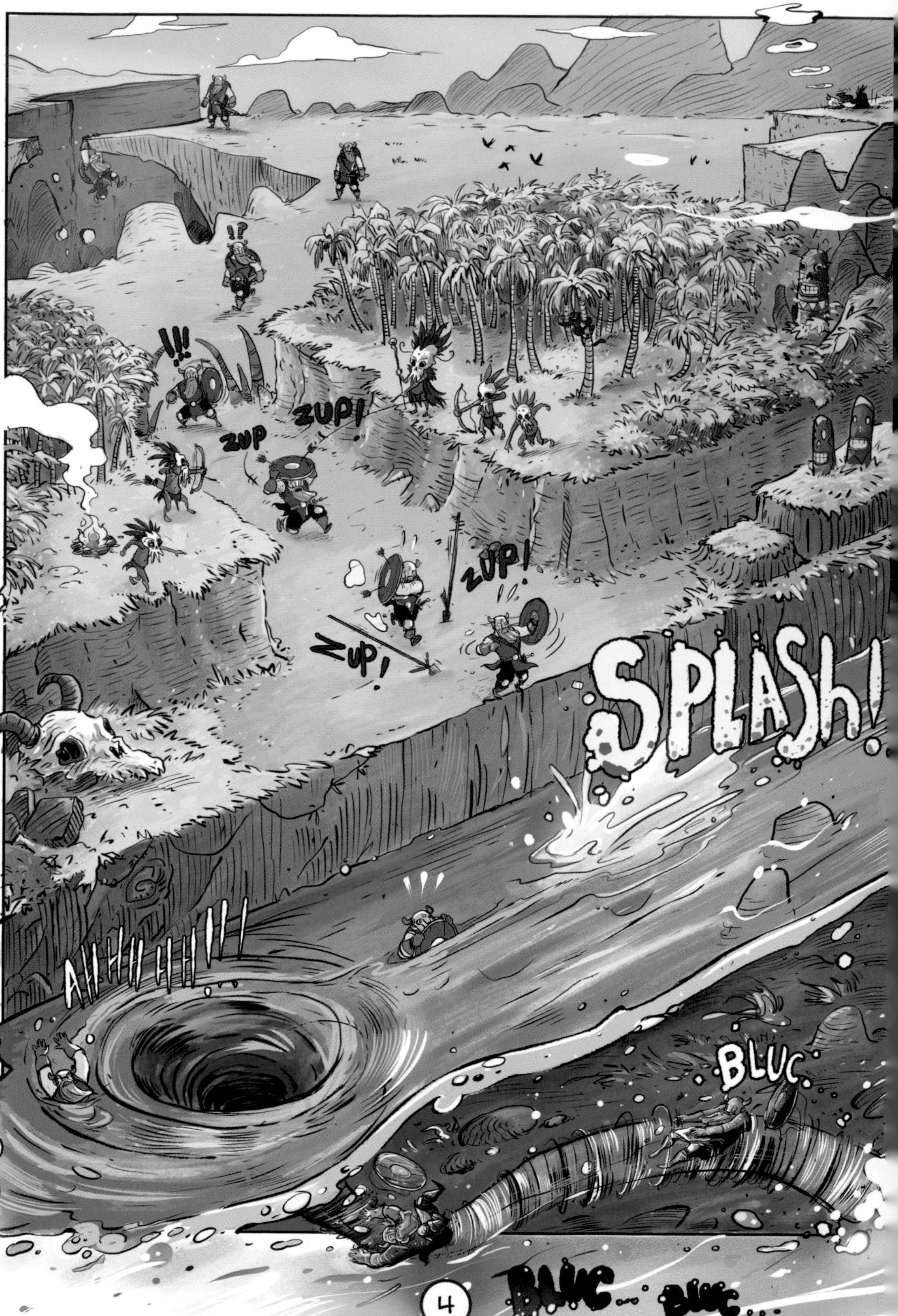
!?
!!!
ZUP!
ZUP
ZUP!
ZUP!
SPLASh!
!!
AHHHHHHH!!!
BLUC
BLUC... BLUC...

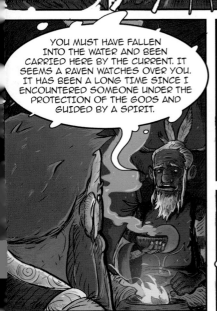

WHO ARE YOU? WHAT HAVE YOU DONE WITH MY THINGS?

EASY, TRAVELER. YOU ARE SAFE... YOUR THINGS ARE RIGHT HERE. I SAW HOW YOU FOUGHT YOUR WAY INTO THE LANDS OF THE ZUARS. YOU WERE SAVED BY GOOD LUCK AND A STRONG SHIELD.

NOOOOOOON!!

YOU MUST HAVE FALLEN INTO THE WATER AND BEEN CARRIED HERE BY THE CURRENT. IT SEEMS A RAVEN WATCHES OVER YOU. IT HAS BEEN A LONG TIME SINCE I ENCOUNTERED SOMEONE UNDER THE PROTECTION OF THE GODS AND GUIDED BY A SPIRIT.

HERE, DRINK THIS. IT WILL EASE YOUR FEVER BEFORE YOU CONTINUE ON YOUR JOURNEY.

SLURP

YOU MUST TAKE CARE IN CHOOSING YOUR PATH. IT IS OF THE GREATEST IMPORTANCE. FOLLOW ME...

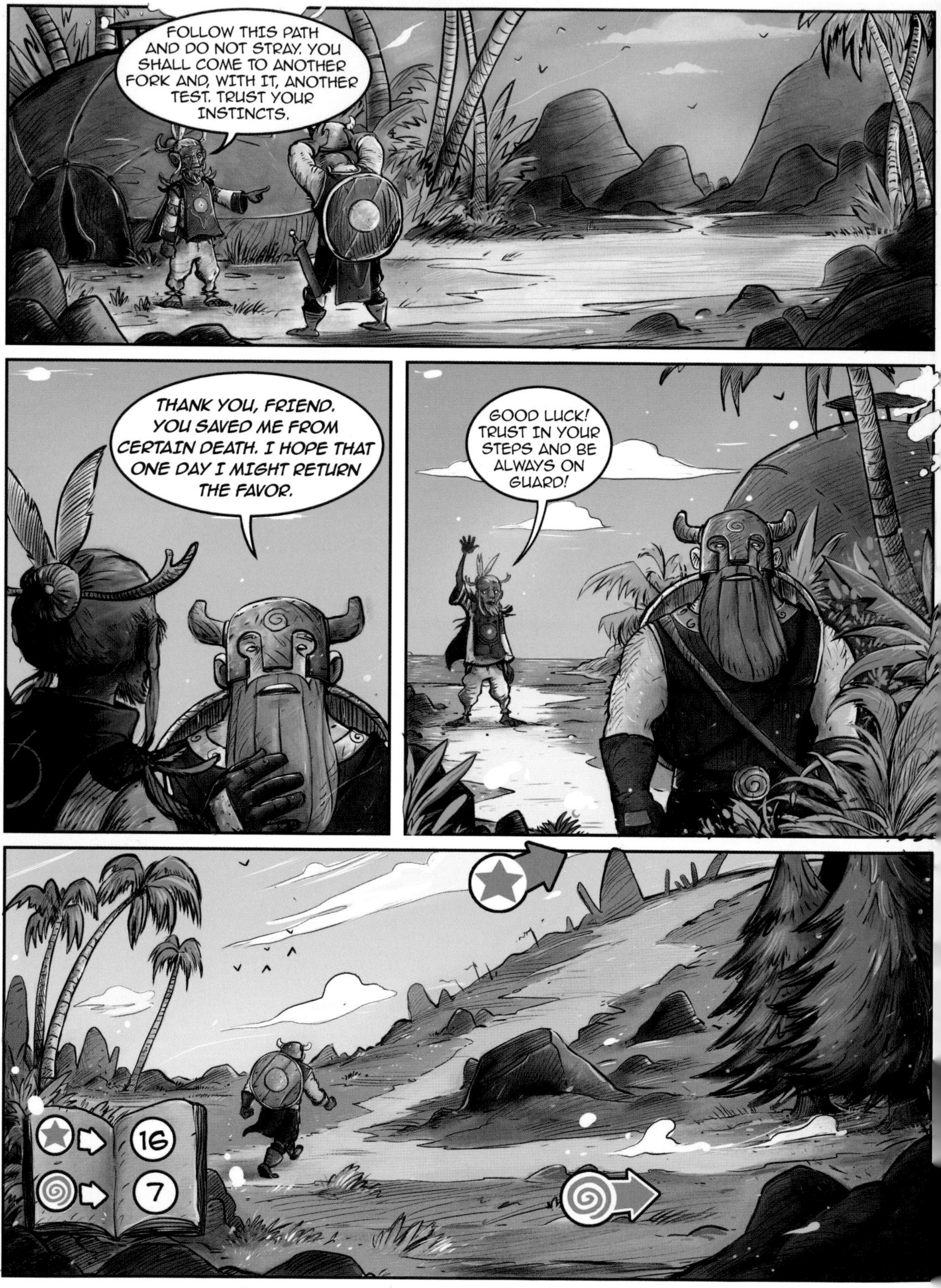
FOLLOW THIS PATH AND DO NOT STRAY. YOU SHALL COME TO ANOTHER FORK AND, WITH IT, ANOTHER TEST. TRUST YOUR INSTINCTS.
THANK YOU, FRIEND. YOU SAVED ME FROM CERTAIN DEATH. I HOPE THAT ONE DAY I MIGHT RETURN THE FAVOR.
GOOD LUCK! TRUST IN YOUR STEPS AND BE ALWAYS ON GUARD!
16
7

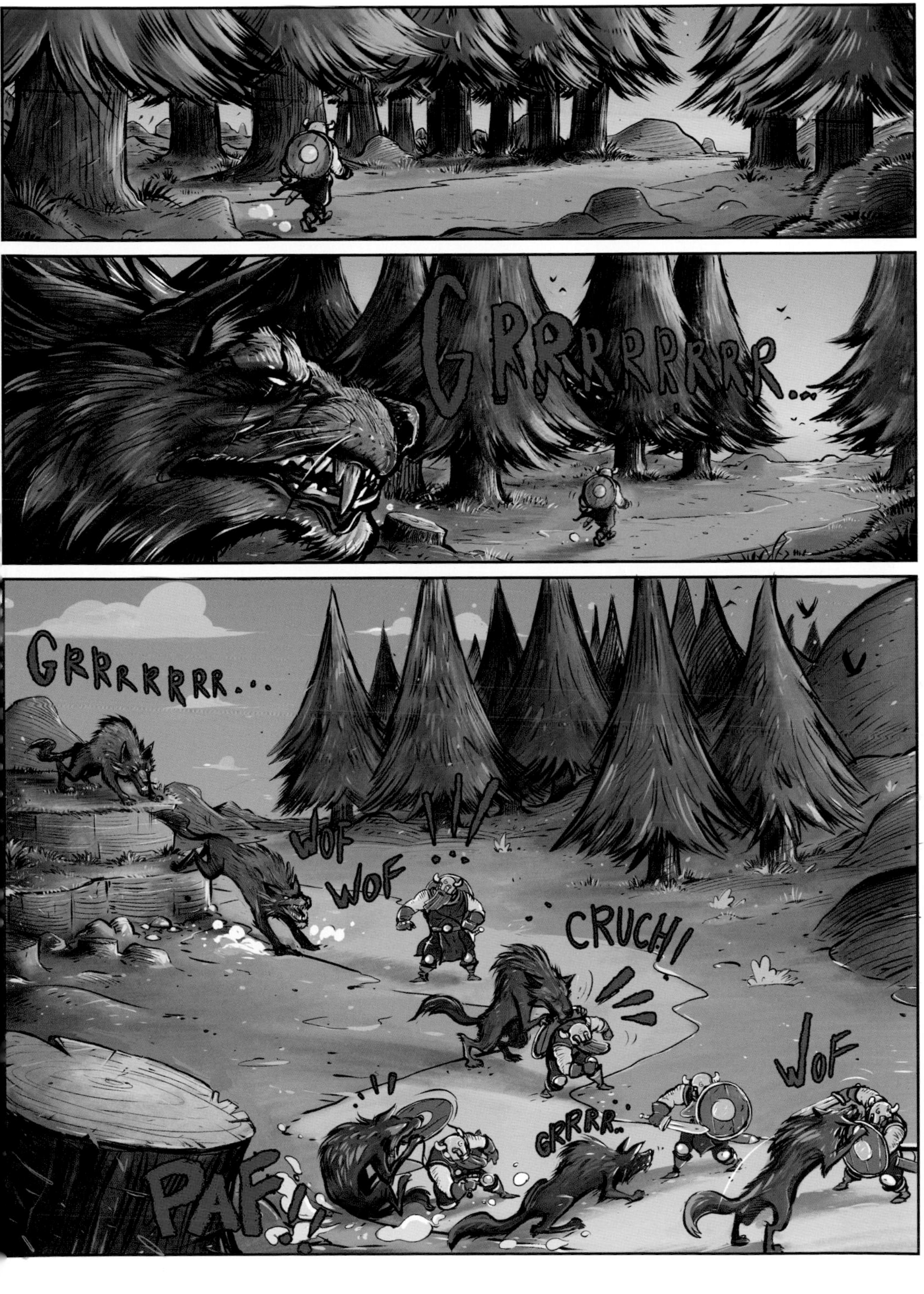
GRRRRRRRRR...
GRRRRRRR...
WOF
WOF
CRUCH!
!!
WOF
GRRRR..
PAF!!

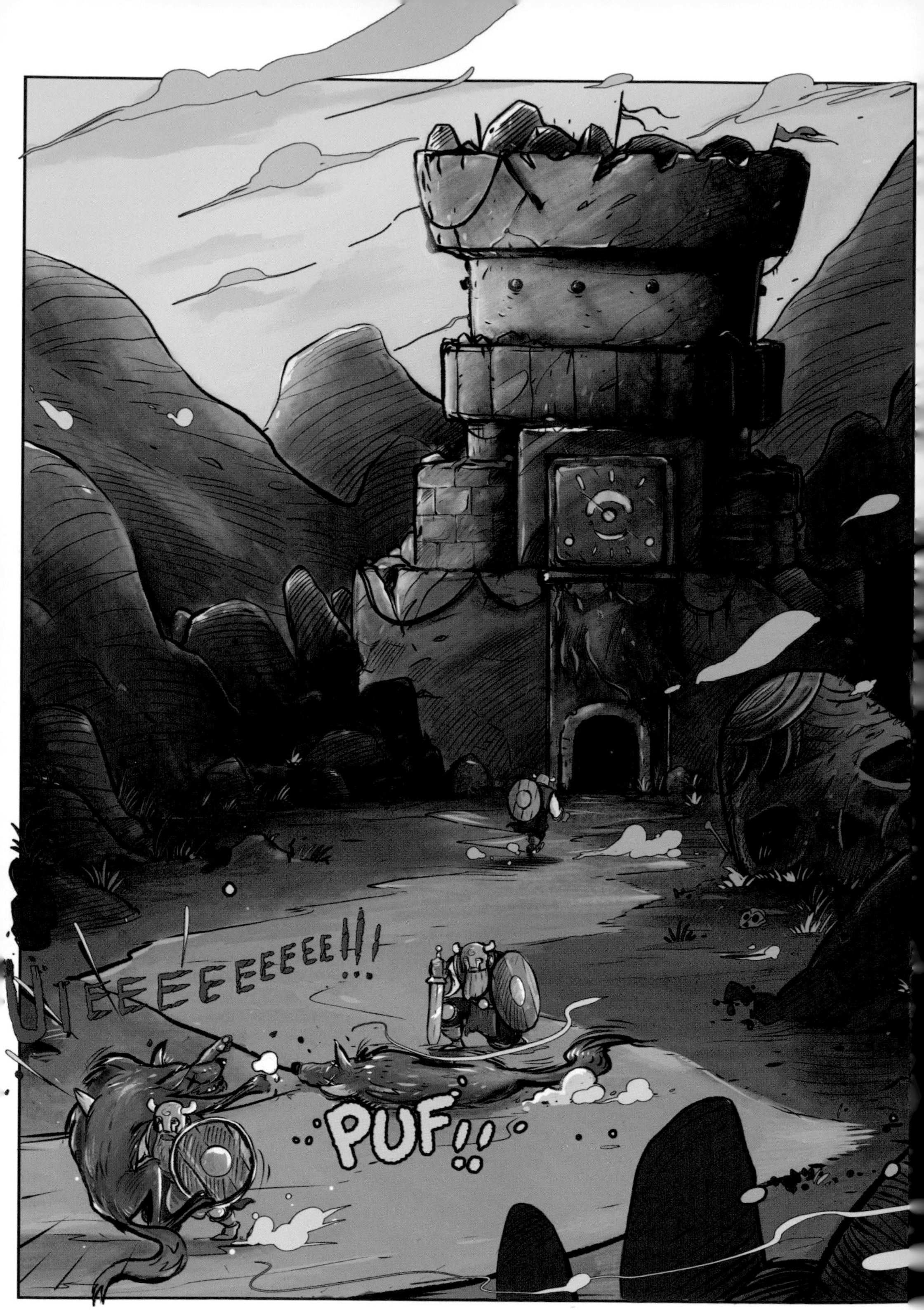
UIEEEEEEEEE!!!
PUF!!

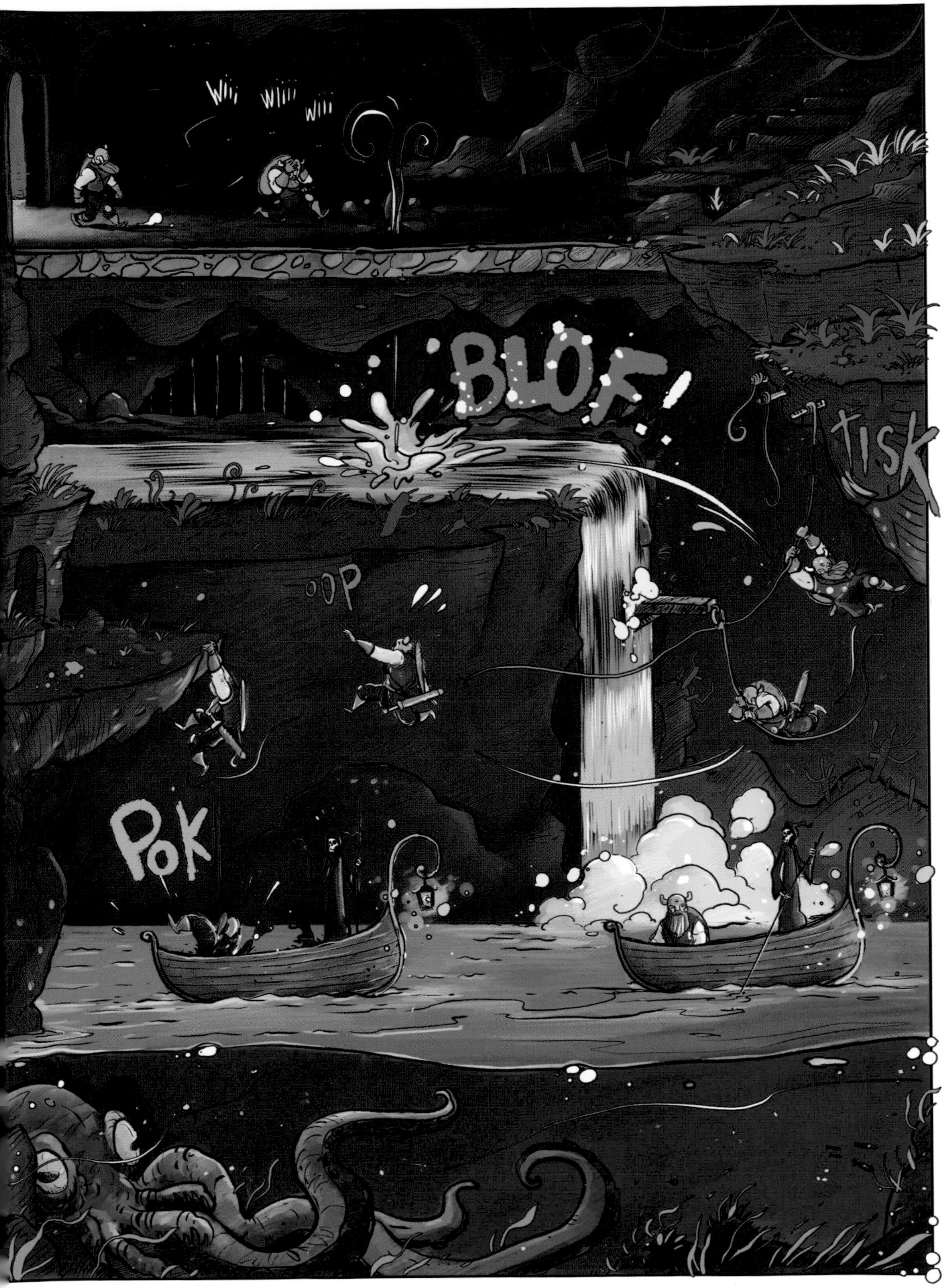
Wiii
Wiiii
Wiii
BLOF!
TISK
OOP
POK

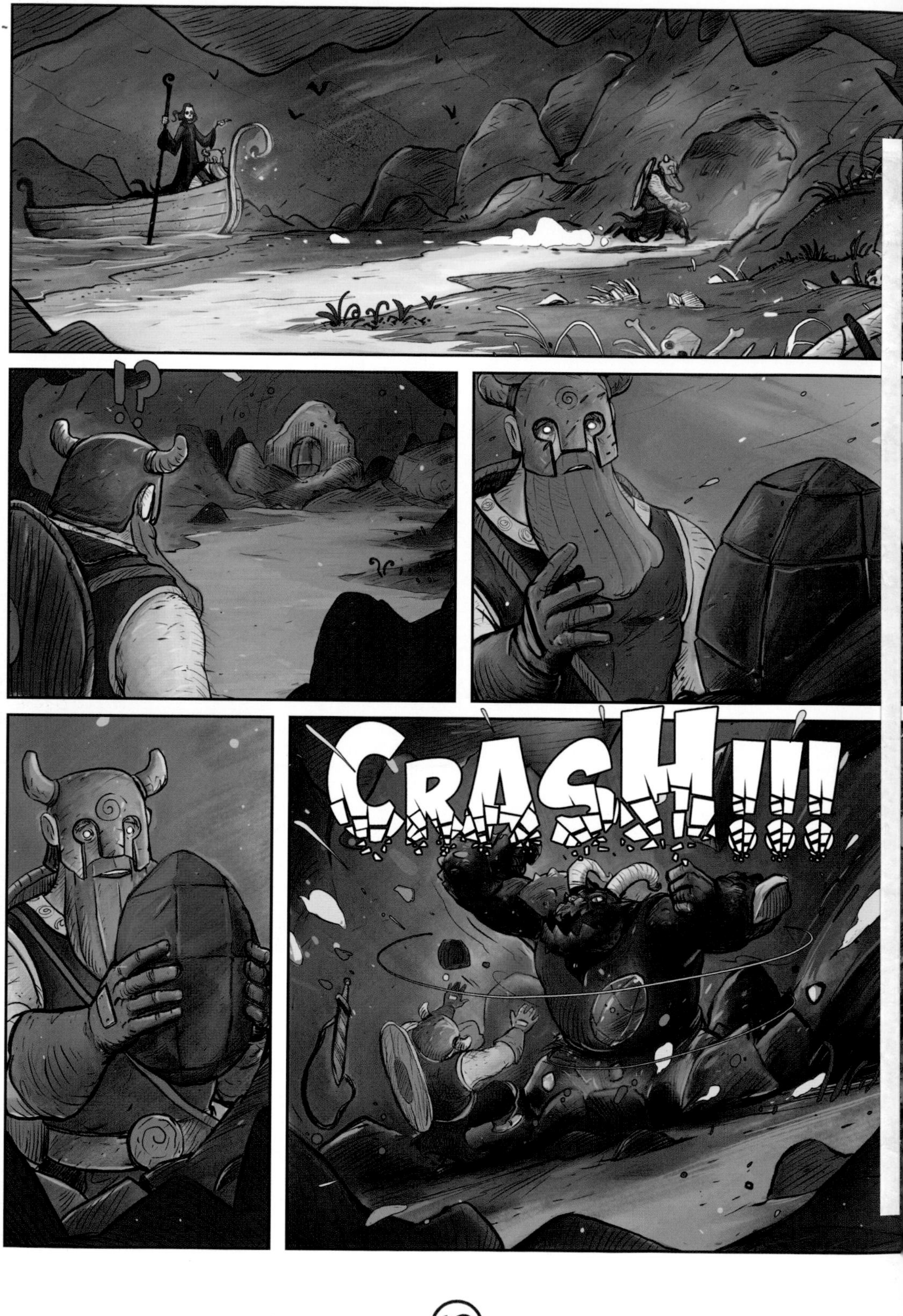
!?
CRASH!!!!

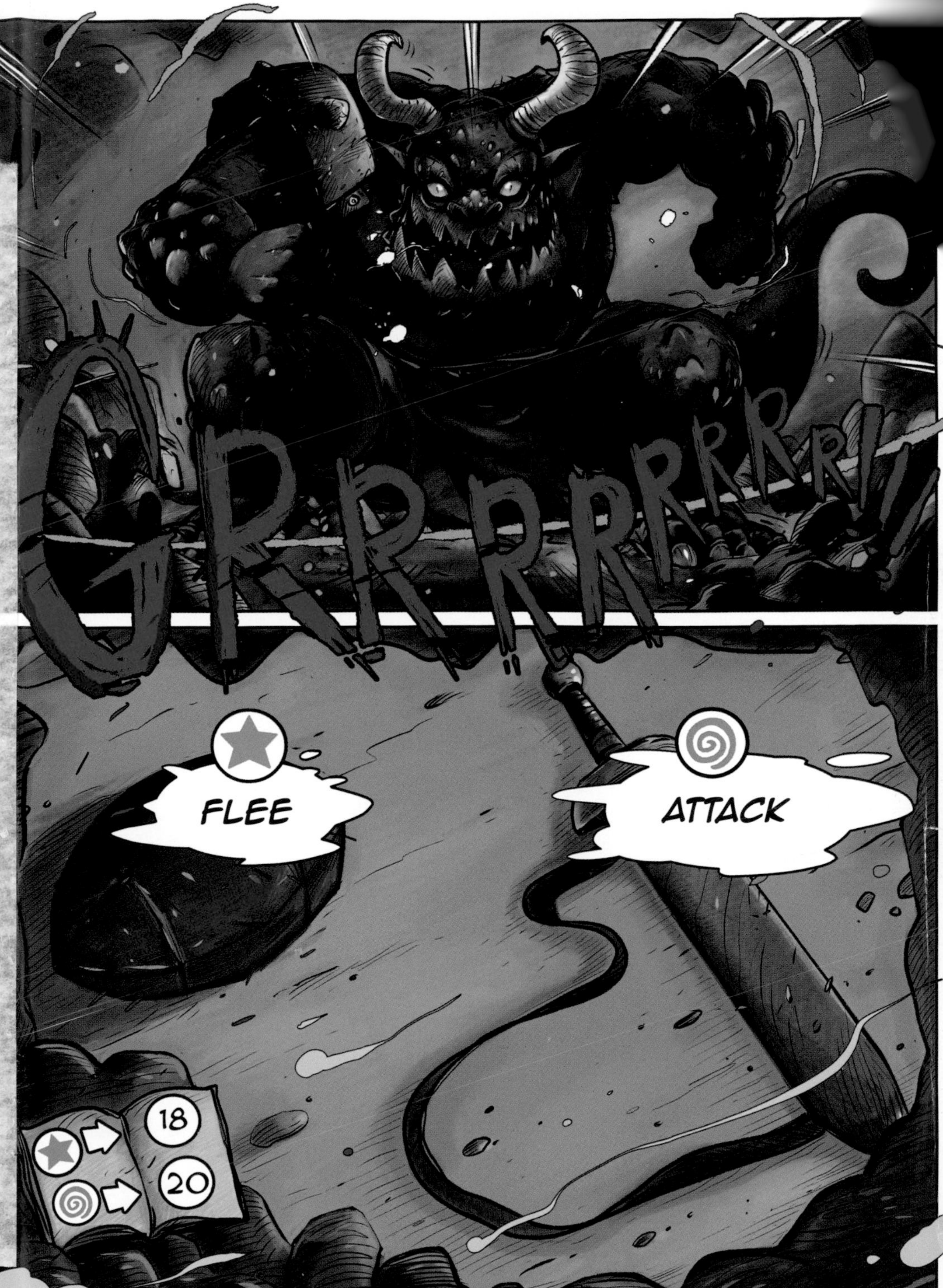
GRRRRRRRRR!!!
FLEE
ATTACK
18
20

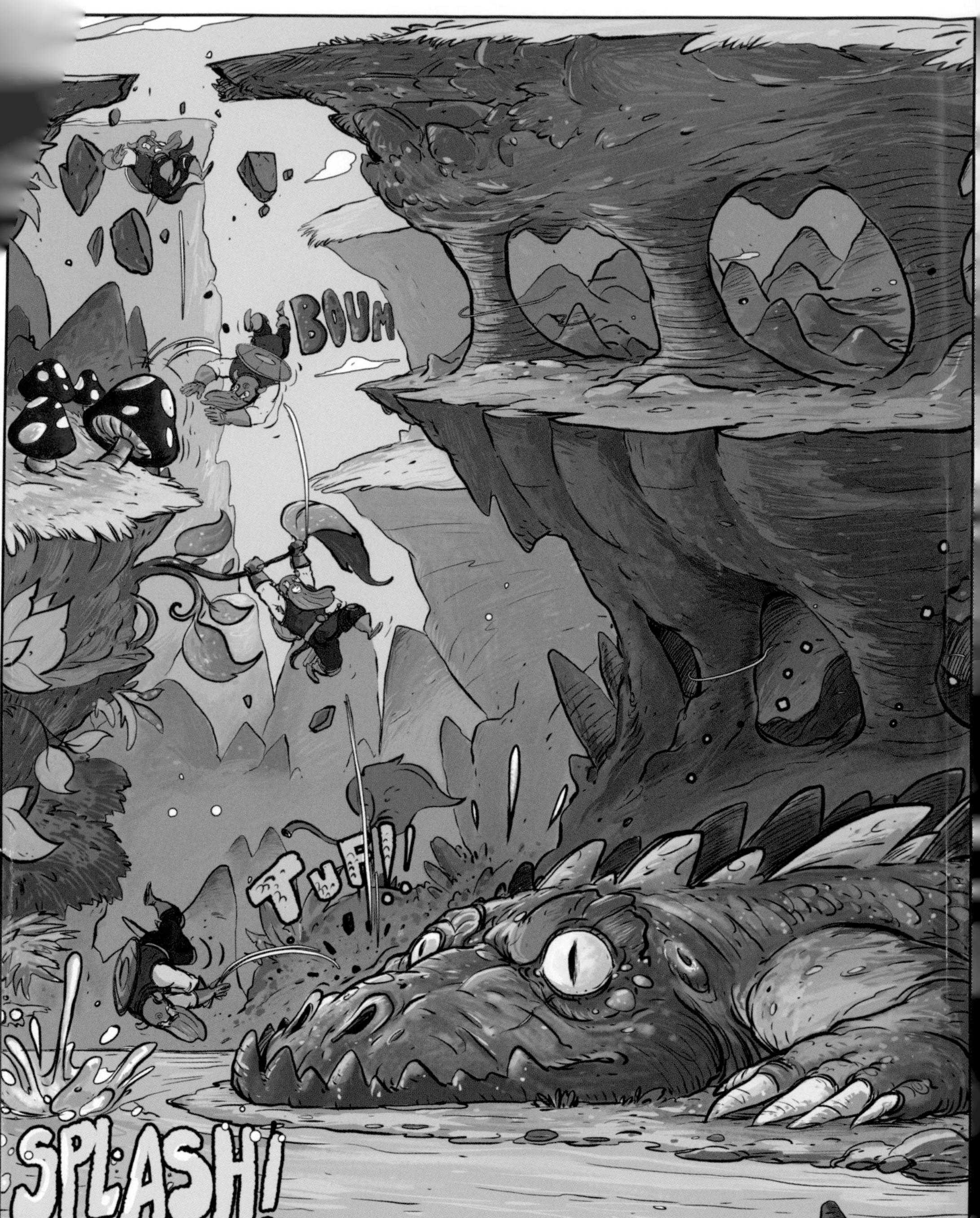
BOUM
TUF!!
SPLASH!

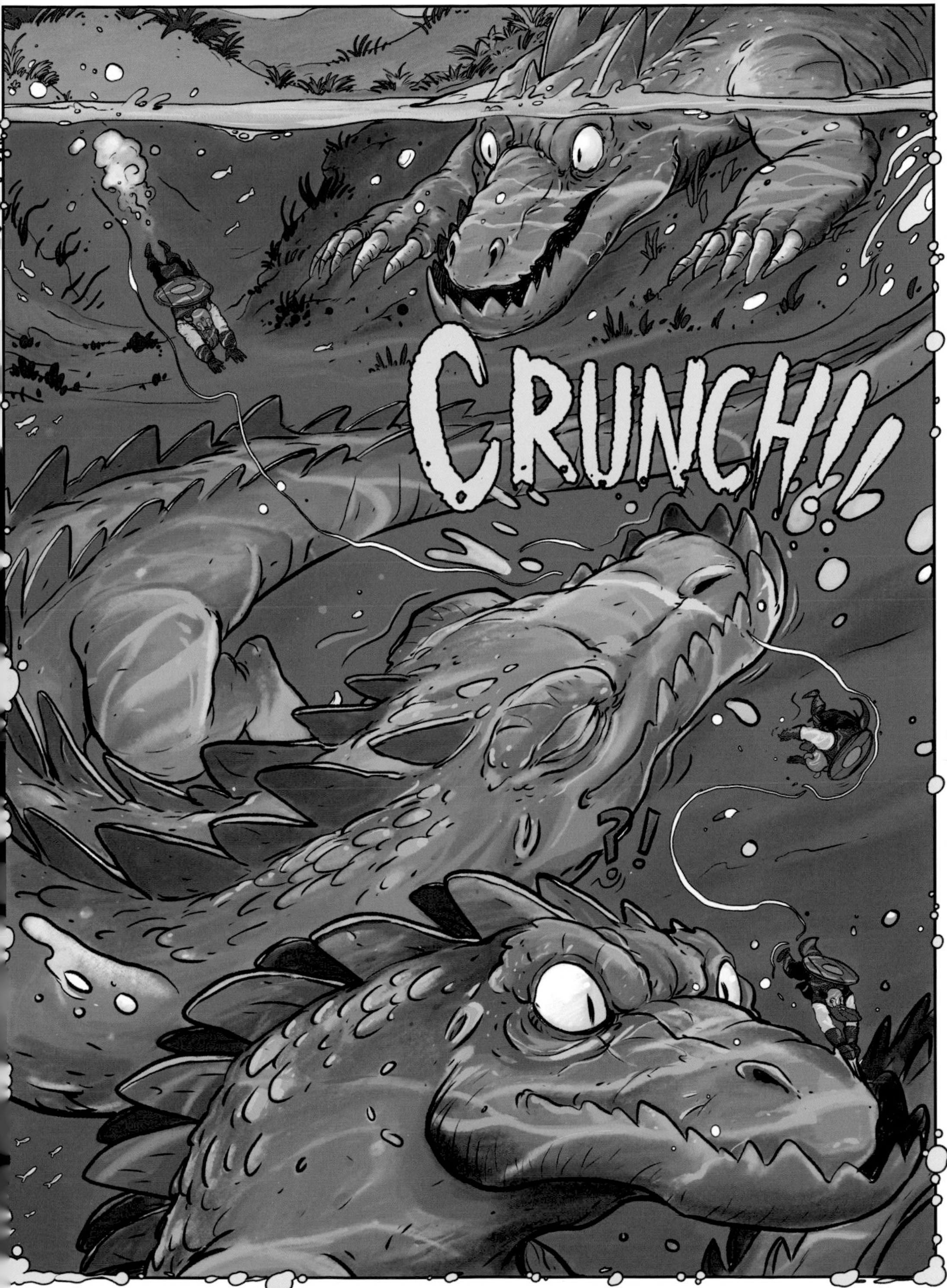
CRUNCH!!
?!

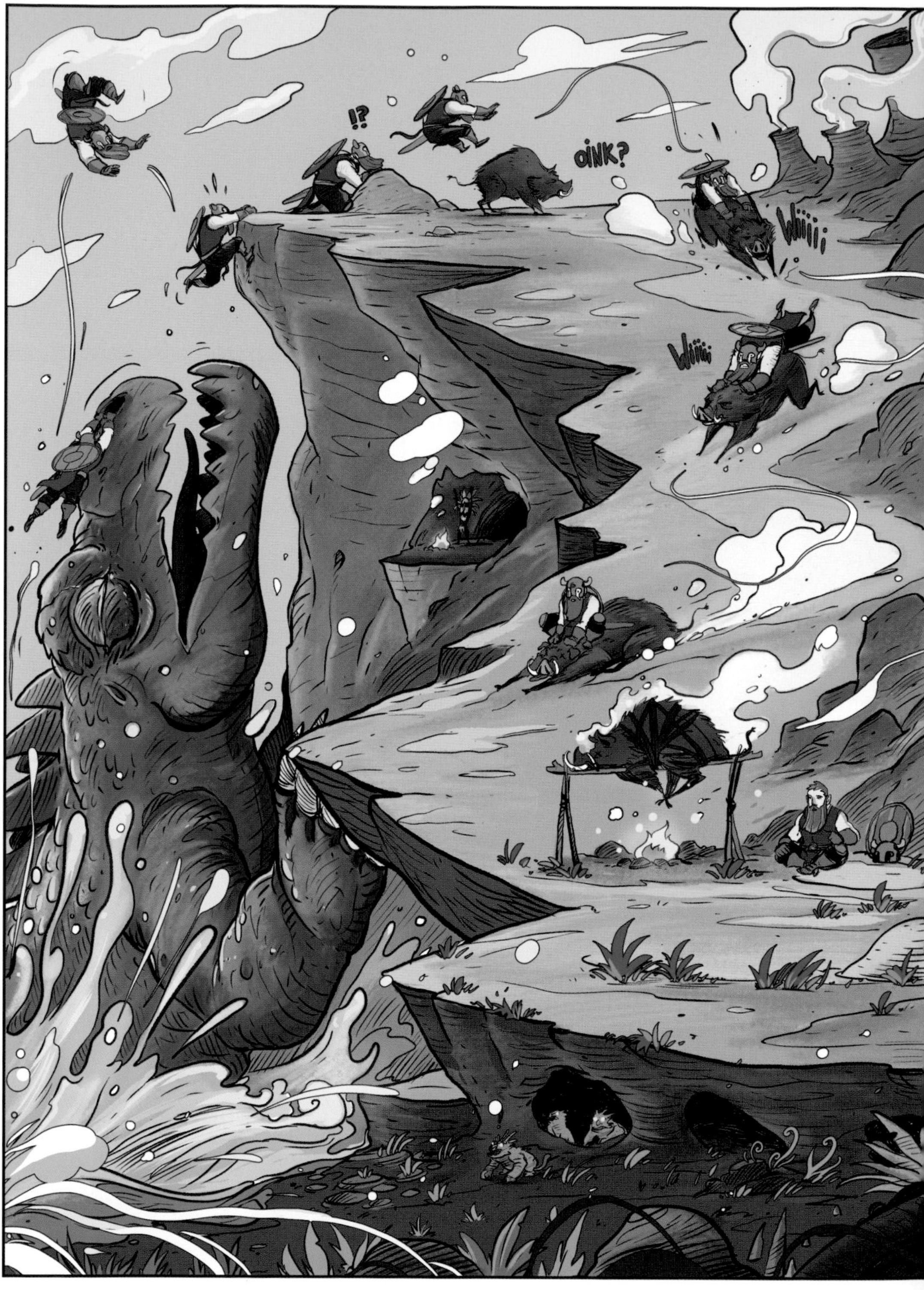
!?
OINK?
Wiiiii
Wiiiii

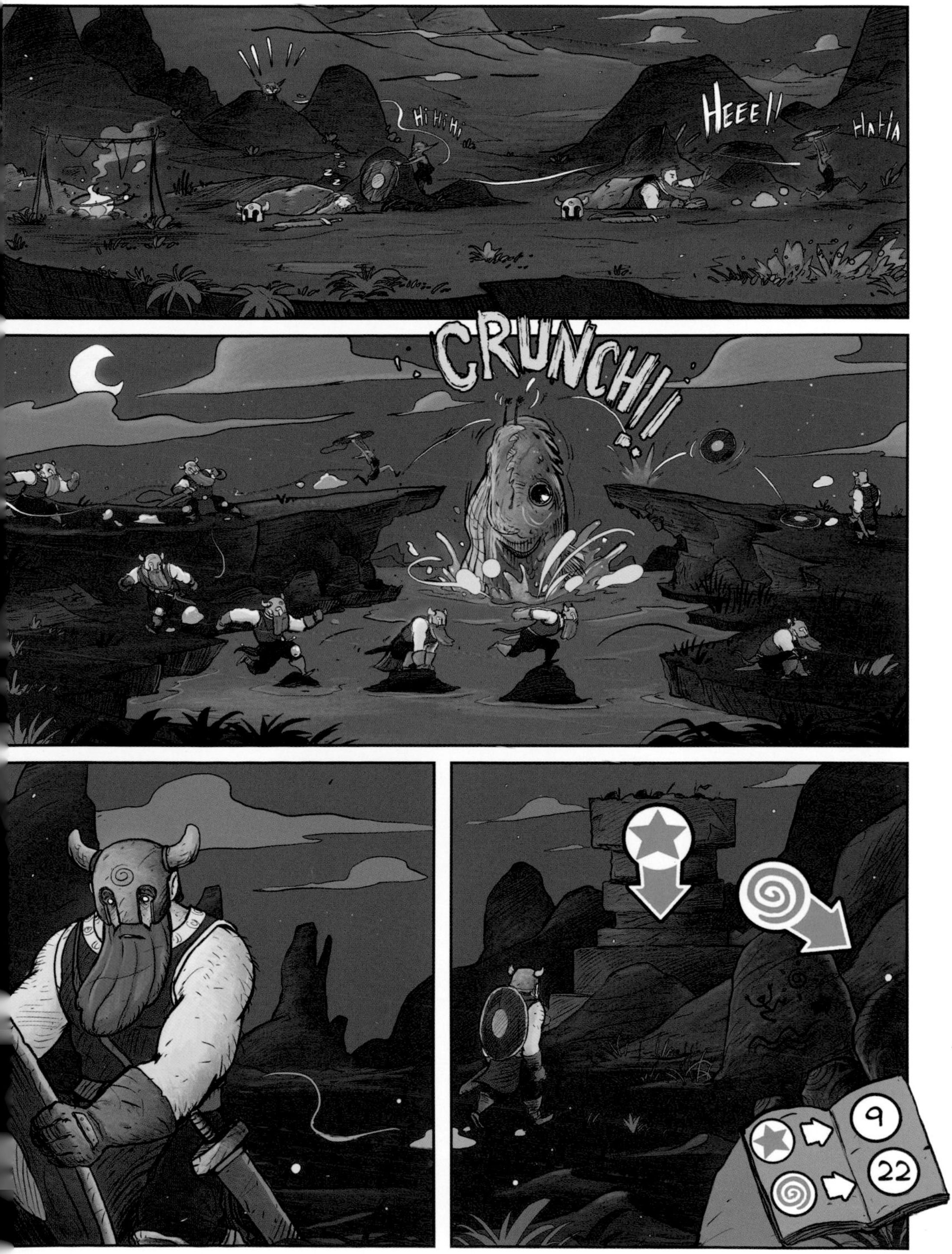
Hi Hi Hi
HEEE!!
HaHa
CRUNCH!!
9
22

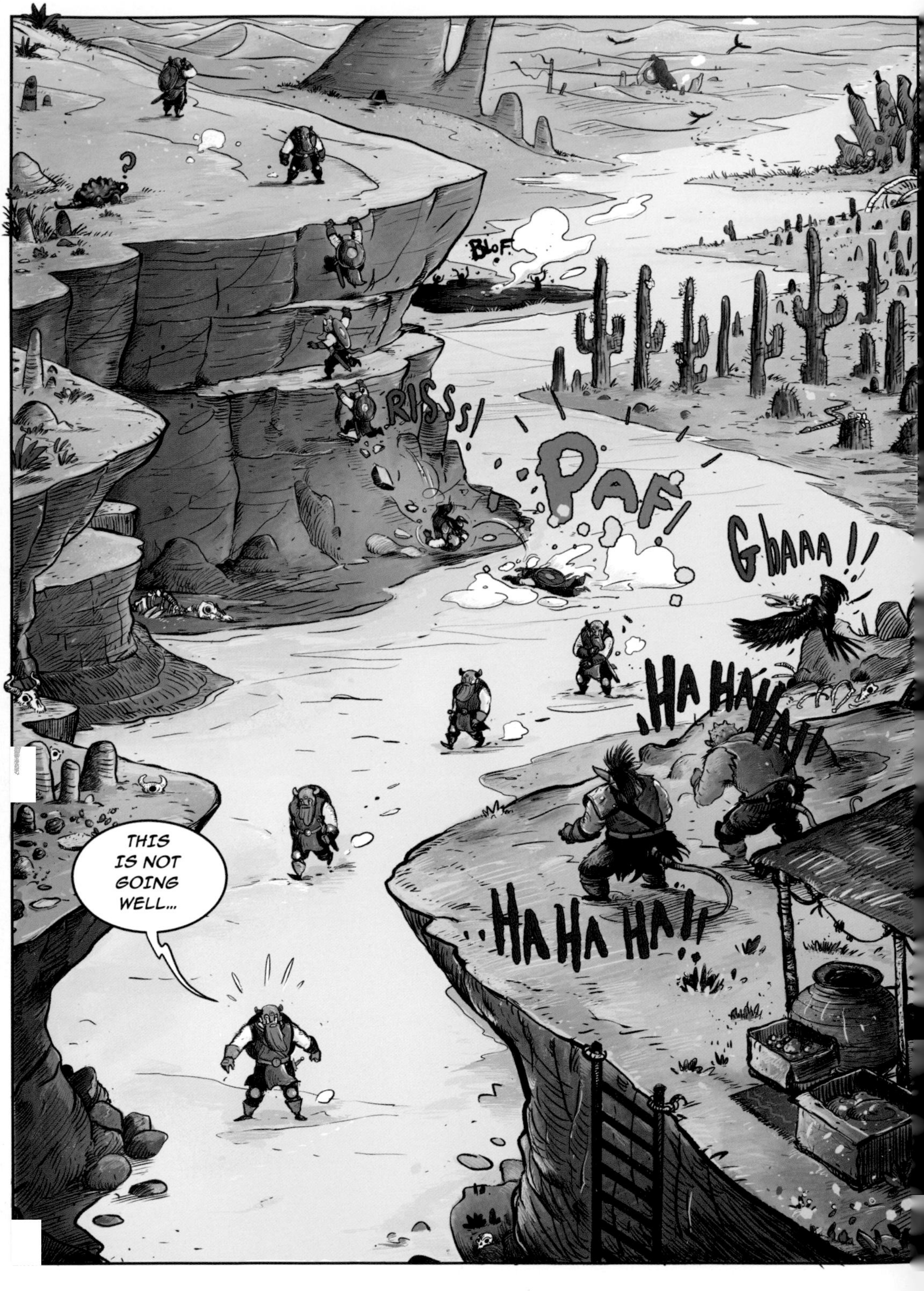
?
BLOF
RISSS!
PAF!
Gbaaa!!
HA HA HA!!
HA HA HA!!
THIS IS NOT GOING WELL...

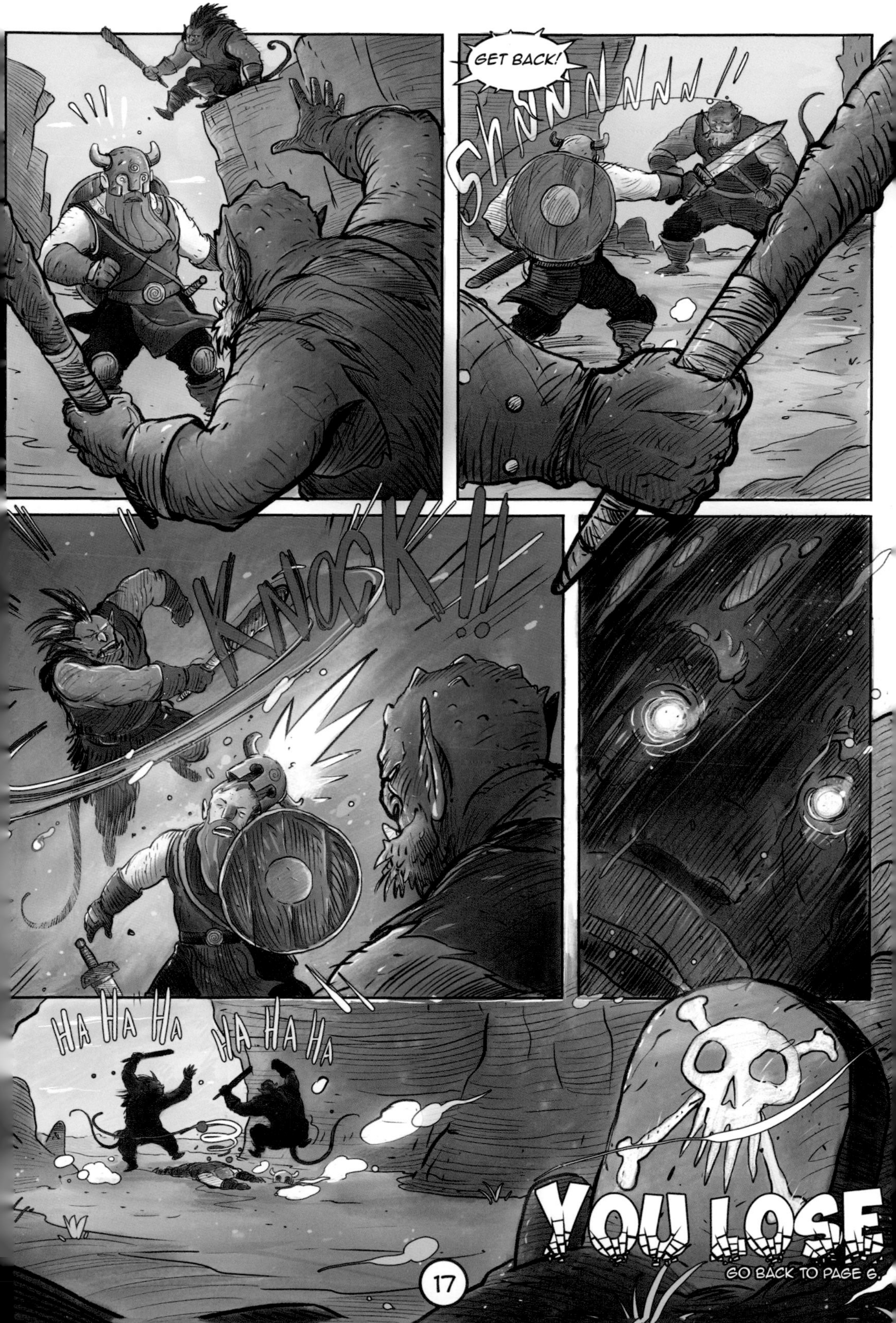
GET BACK!
SHWNNNNNN!!
KNOCK!!
HA HA HA
HA HA HA HA
YOU LOSE
GO BACK TO PAGE 6.

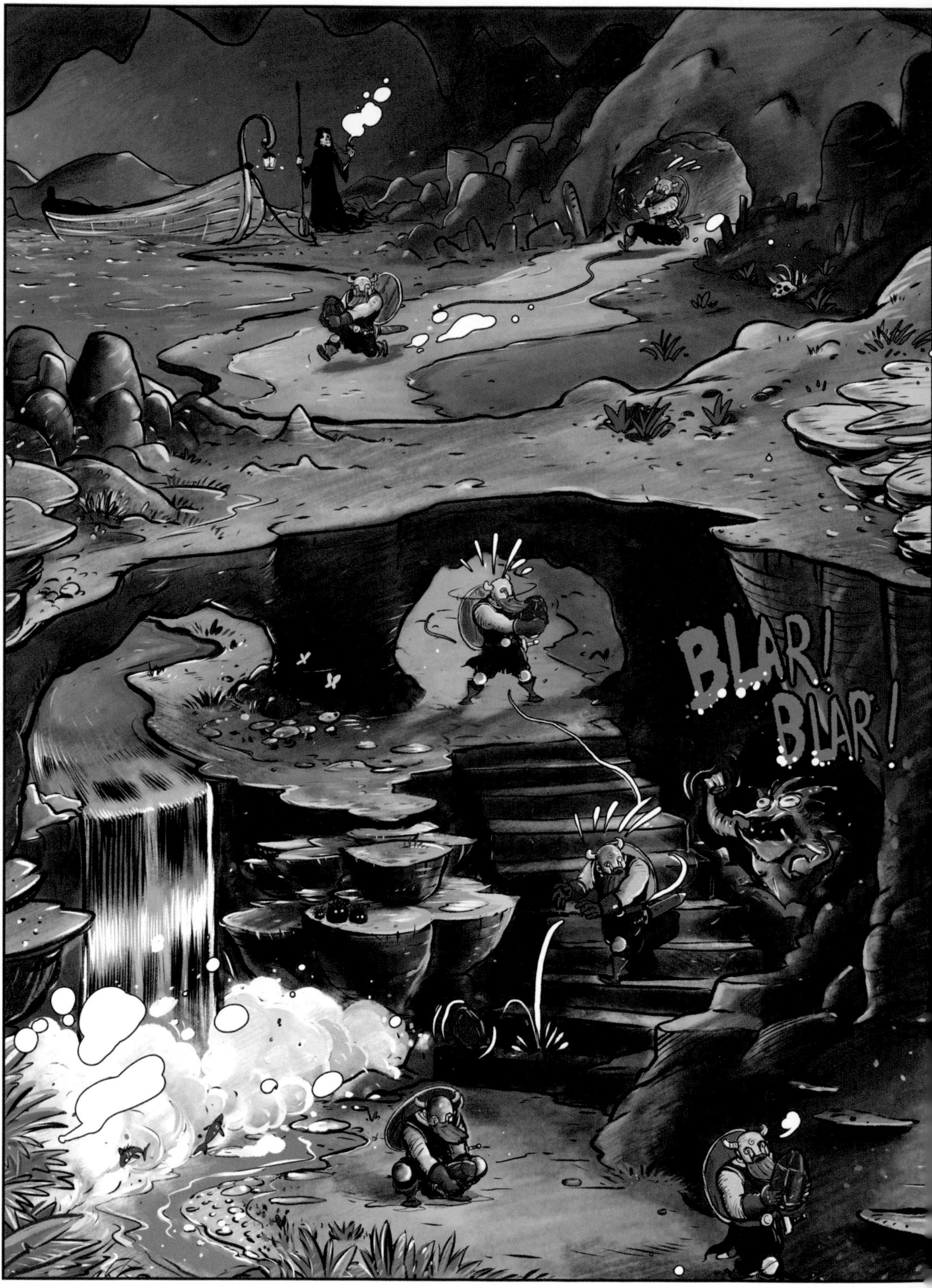
BLAR!
BLAR!

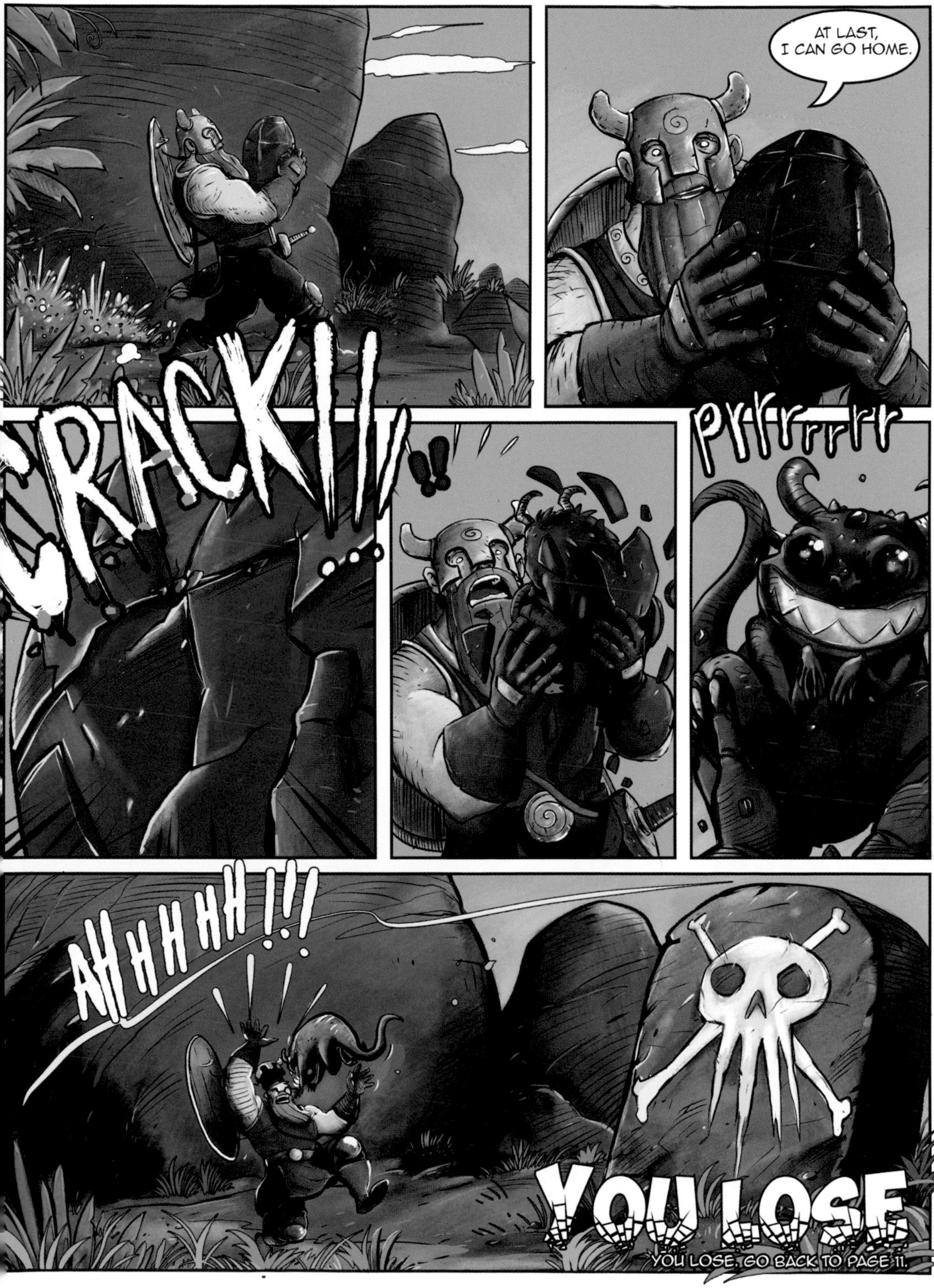
AT LAST, I CAN GO HOME.
CRACK!!
...
!!
prrrrrrr
AHHHHH!!!
YOU LOSE
YOU LOSE. GO BACK TO PAGE 11.

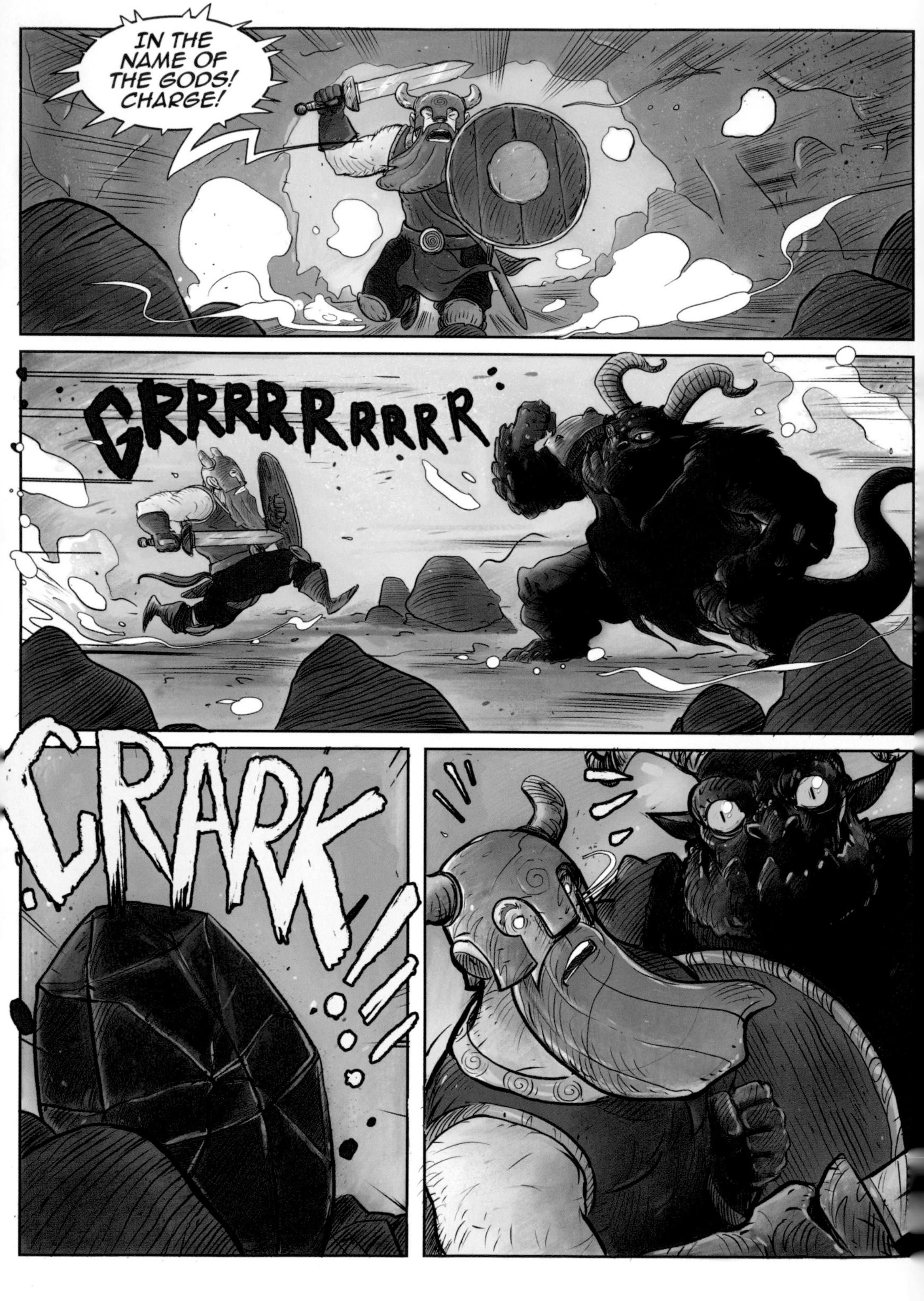
IN THE NAME OF THE GODS! CHARGE!
GRRRRRRRRR
CRARK

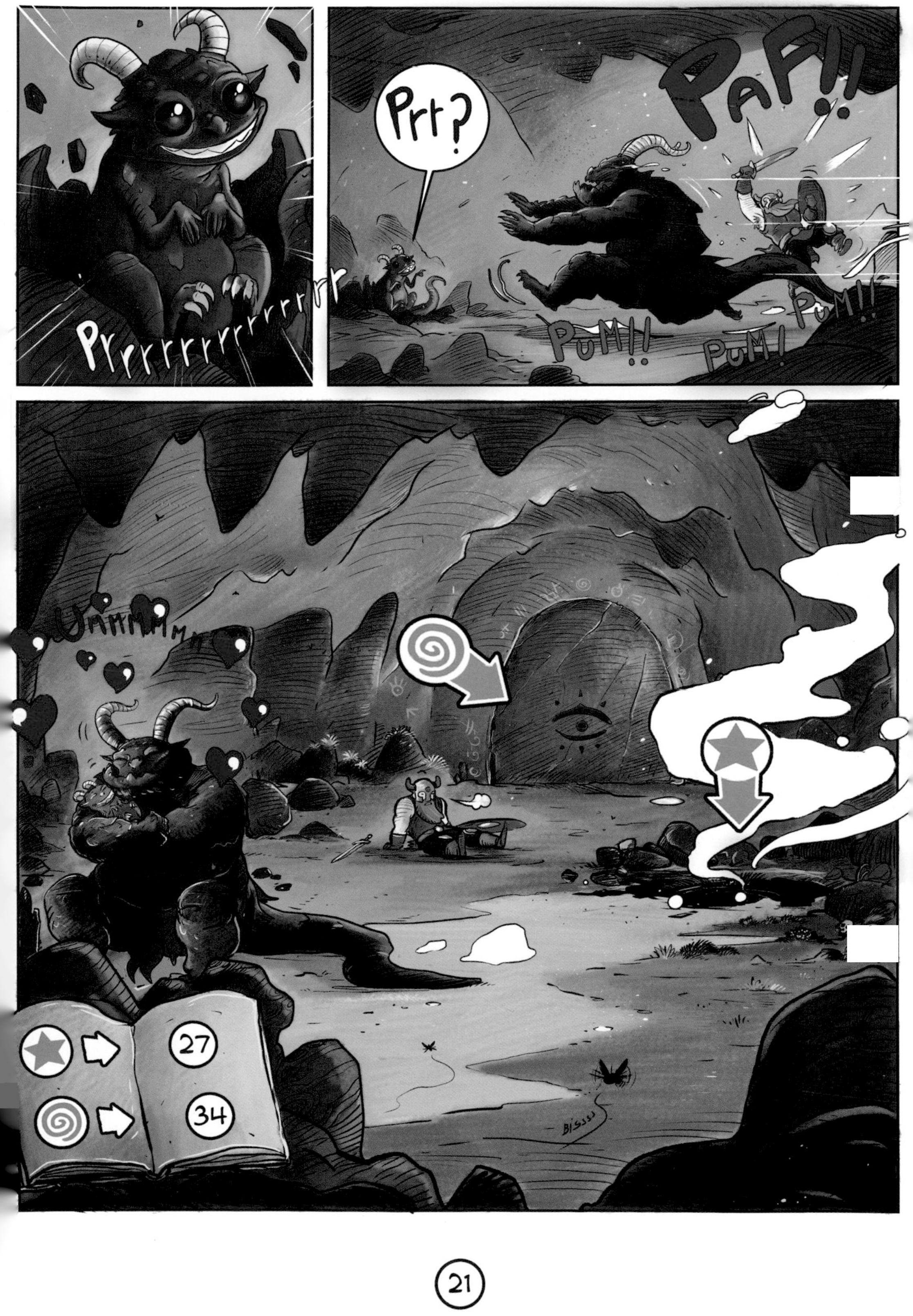
Prrrrrrrrrrrrrr
Prt?
PAF!!
PUM!!
PUM!
PUM!!
UHHMMMm
BISSSS
27
34

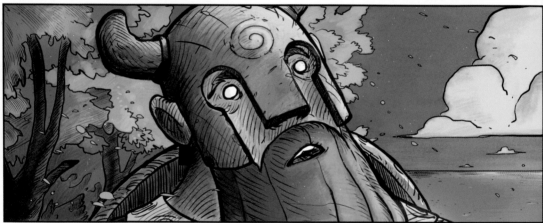

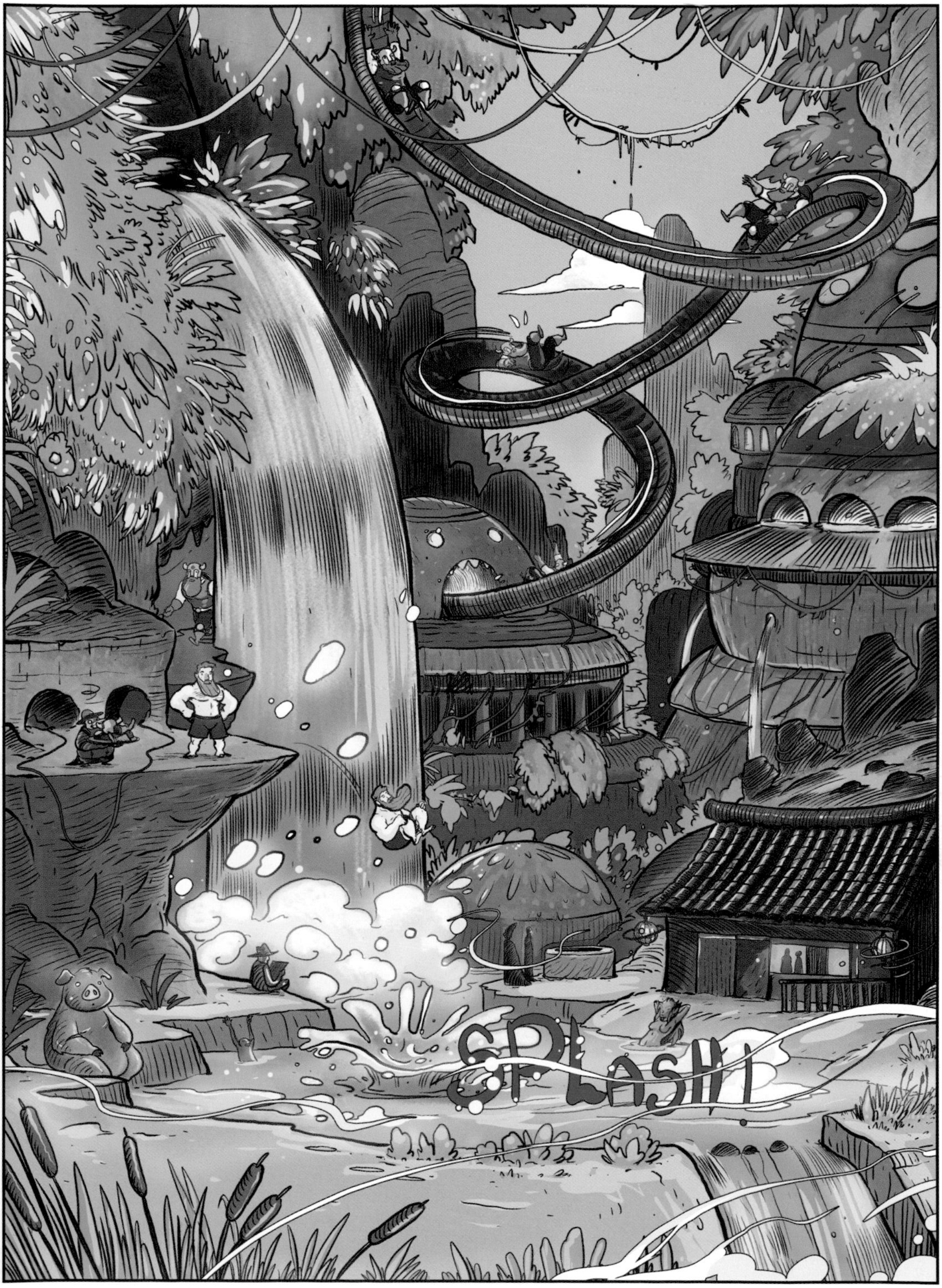
SPLASH!

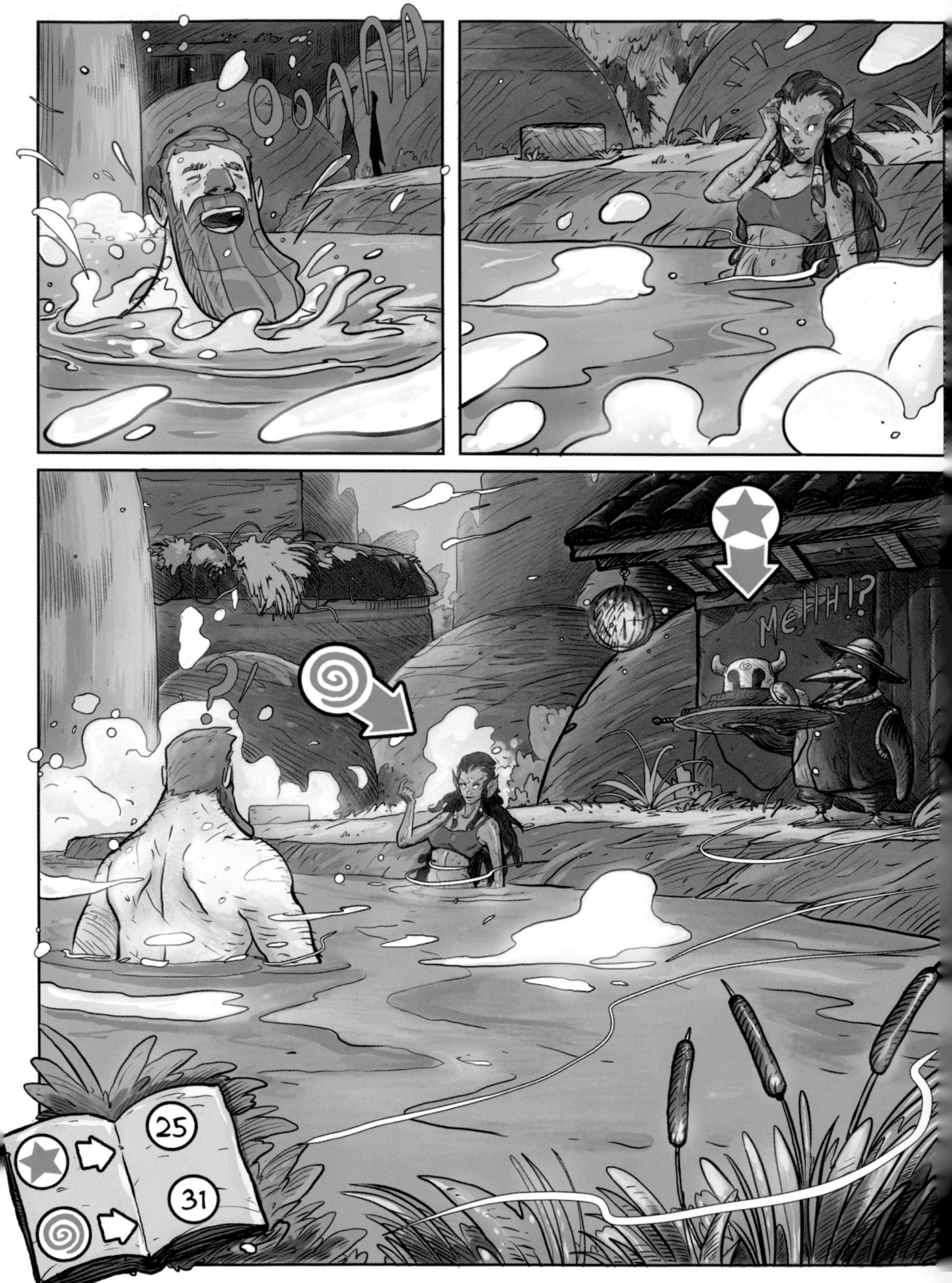
OOAAAA
?!
MEHH!?
25
31

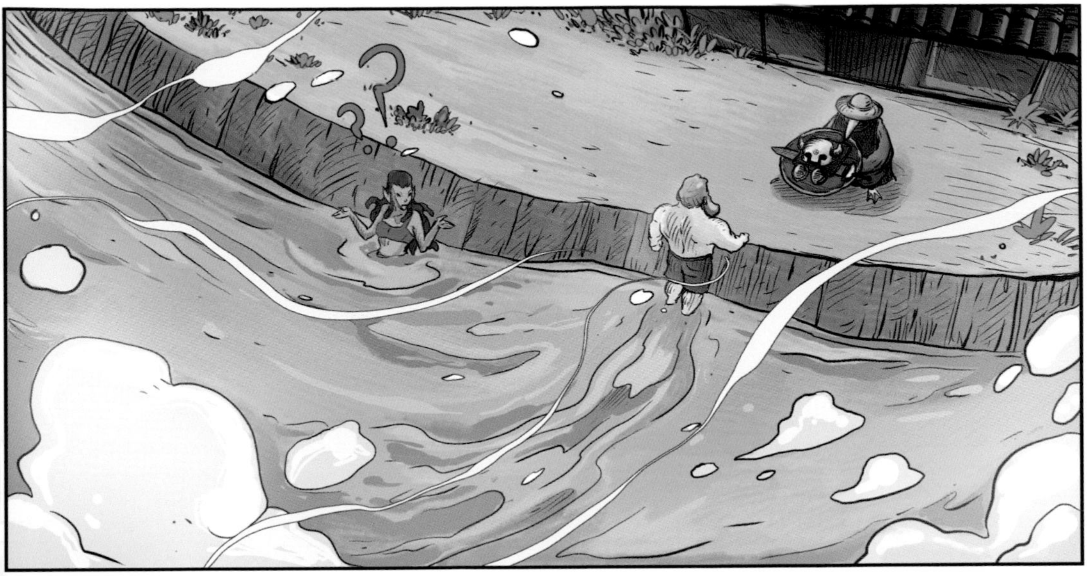

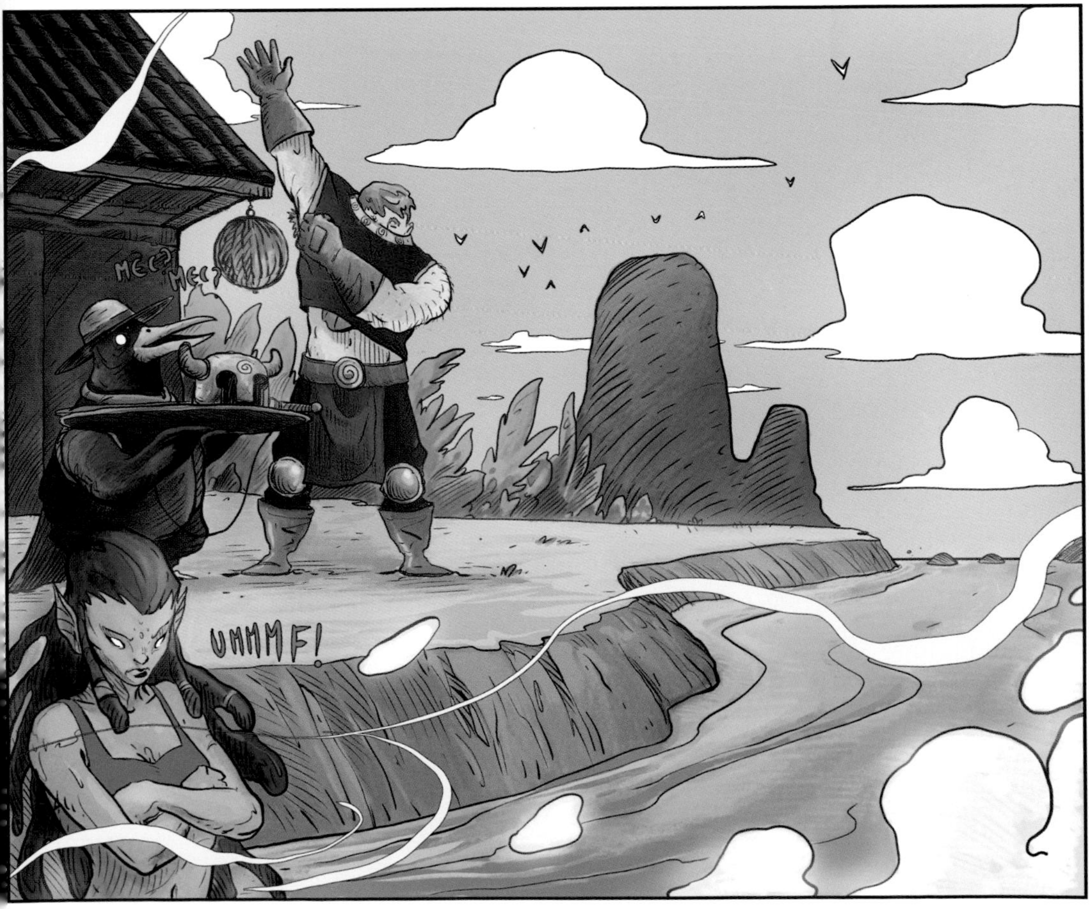
UMMMF!

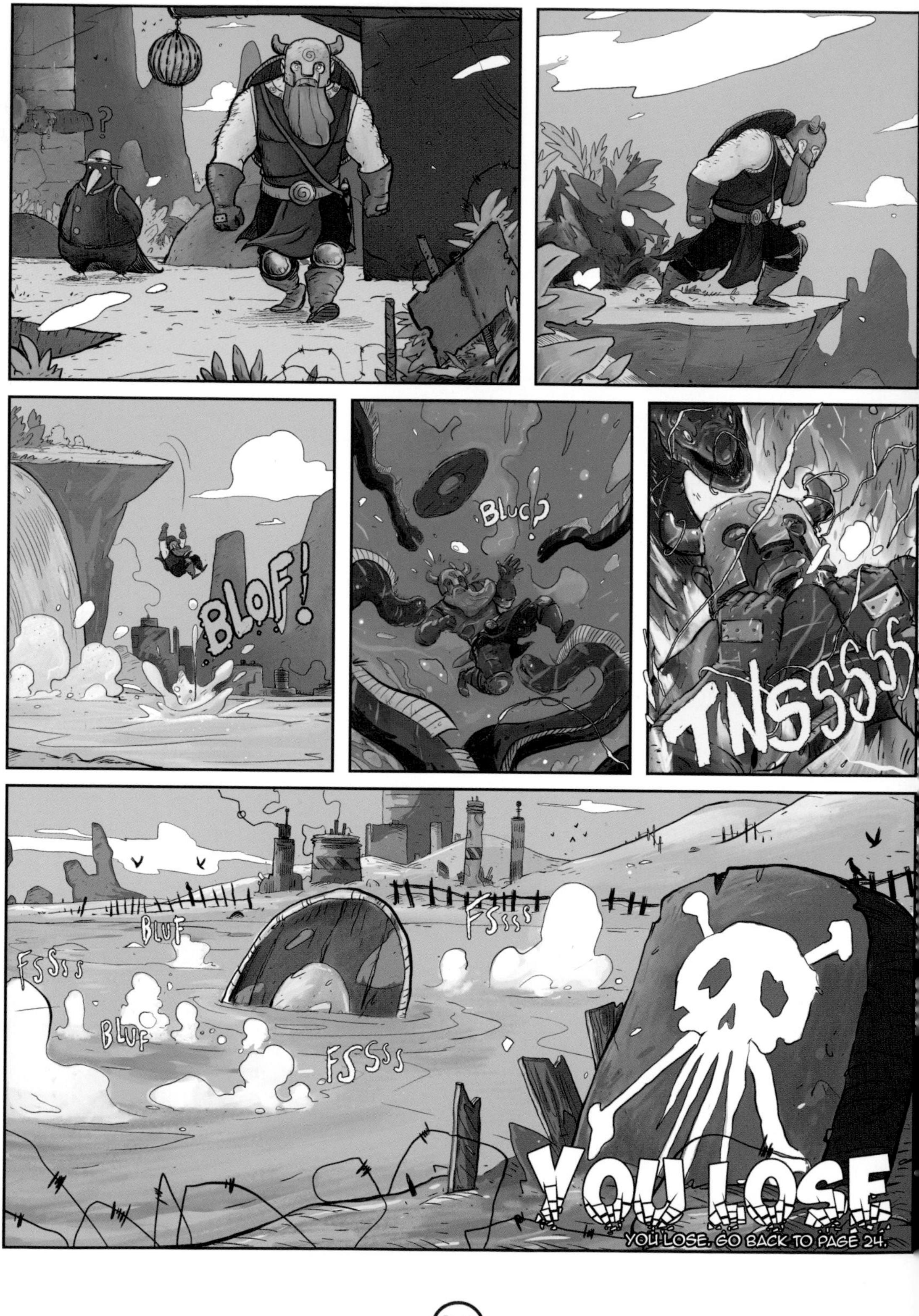
?
BLOF!
Bluc
TNSSSSS
BLUF
FSsss
FSsss
BLUF
FSsss
YOU LOSE
YOU LOSE. GO BACK TO PAGE 24.

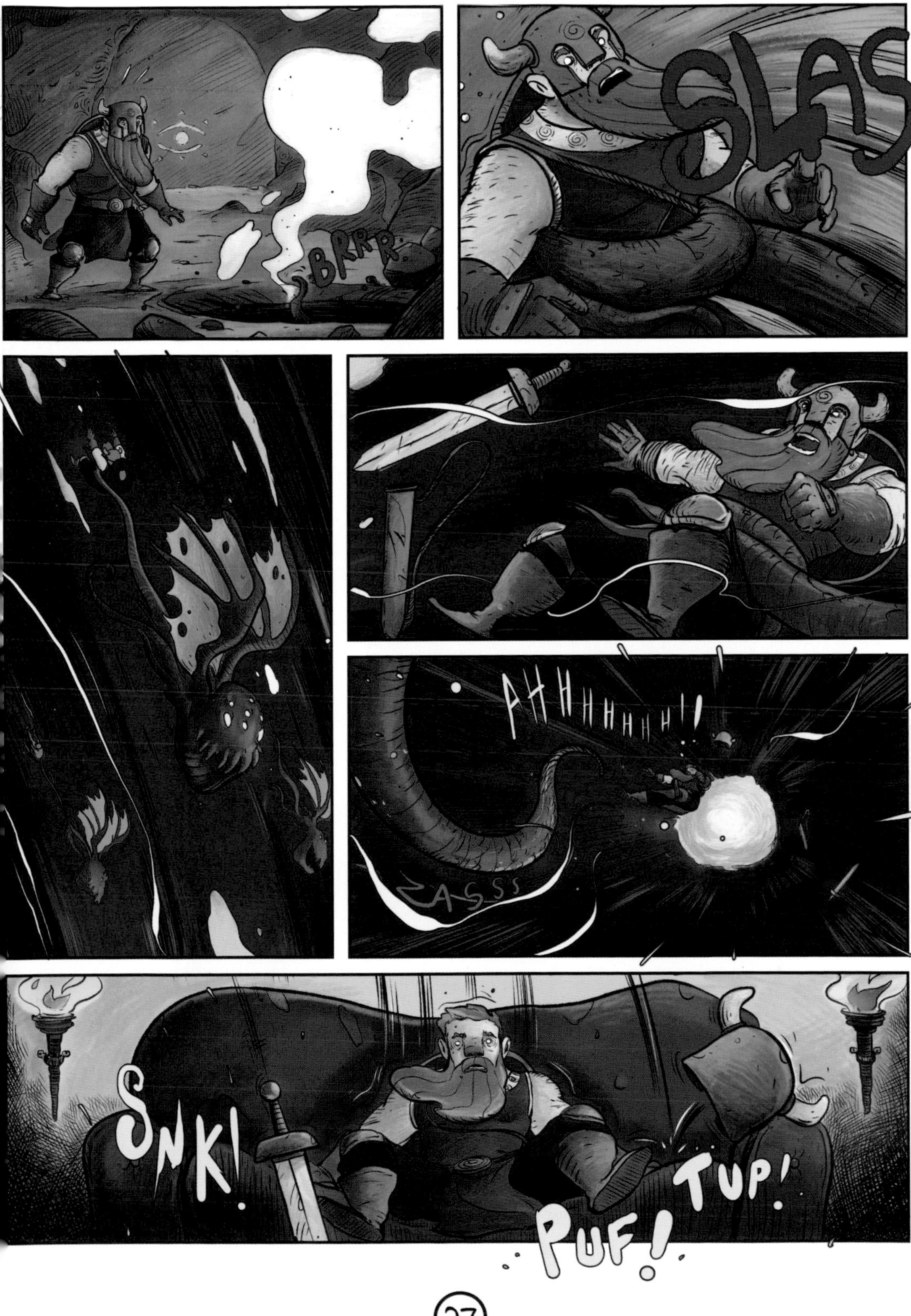
BRRR
SLAS
AHHHHHHH!!
ZASSS
SNK!
TUP!
PUF!

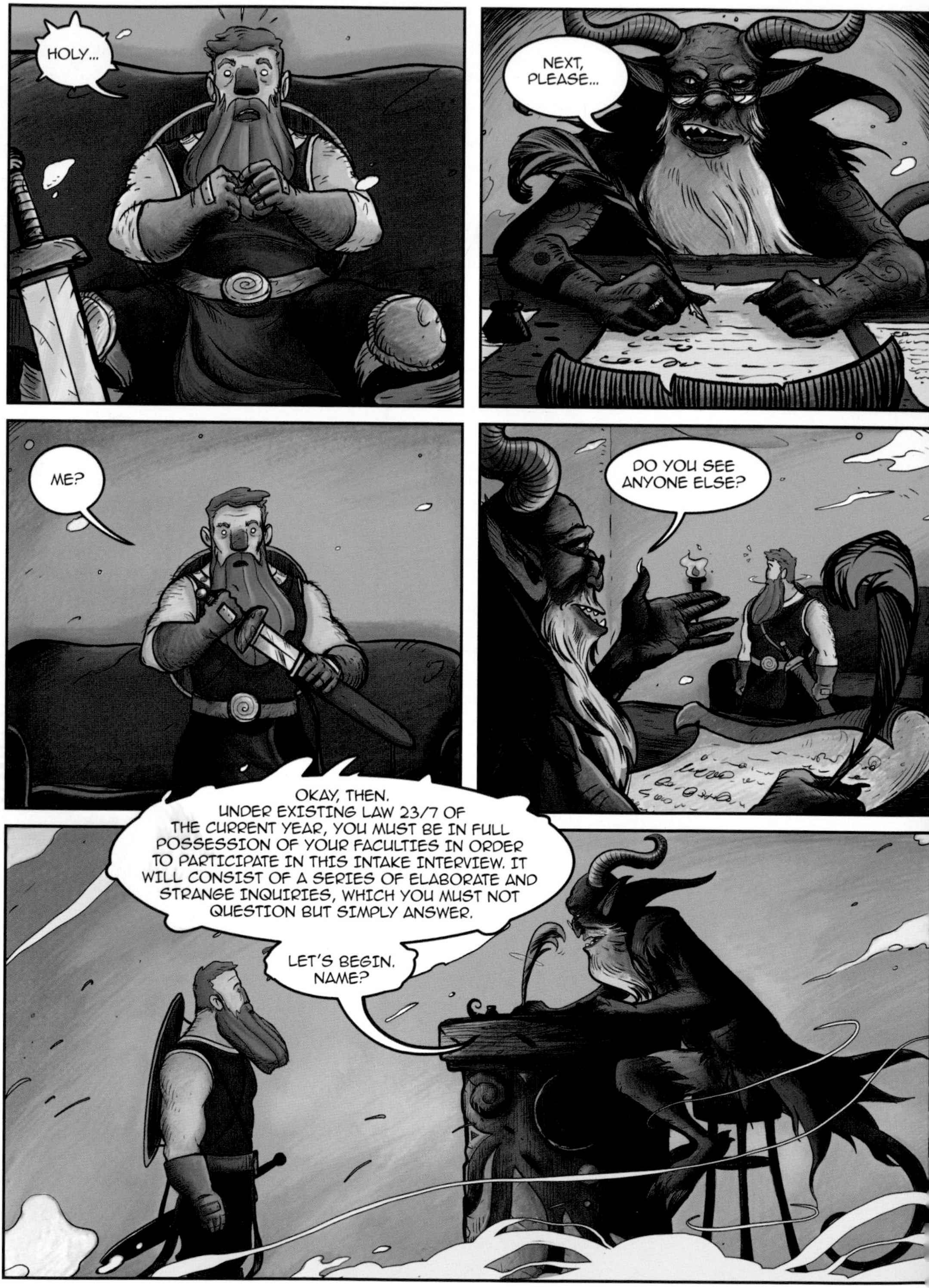
HOLY...
NEXT, PLEASE...
ME?
DO YOU SEE ANYONE ELSE?
OKAY, THEN. UNDER EXISTING LAW 23/7 OF THE CURRENT YEAR, YOU MUST BE IN FULL POSSESSION OF YOUR FACULTIES IN ORDER TO PARTICIPATE IN THIS INTAKE INTERVIEW. IT WILL CONSIST OF A SERIES OF ELABORATE AND STRANGE INQUIRIES, WHICH YOU MUST NOT QUESTION BUT SIMPLY ANSWER.
LET'S BEGIN. NAME?

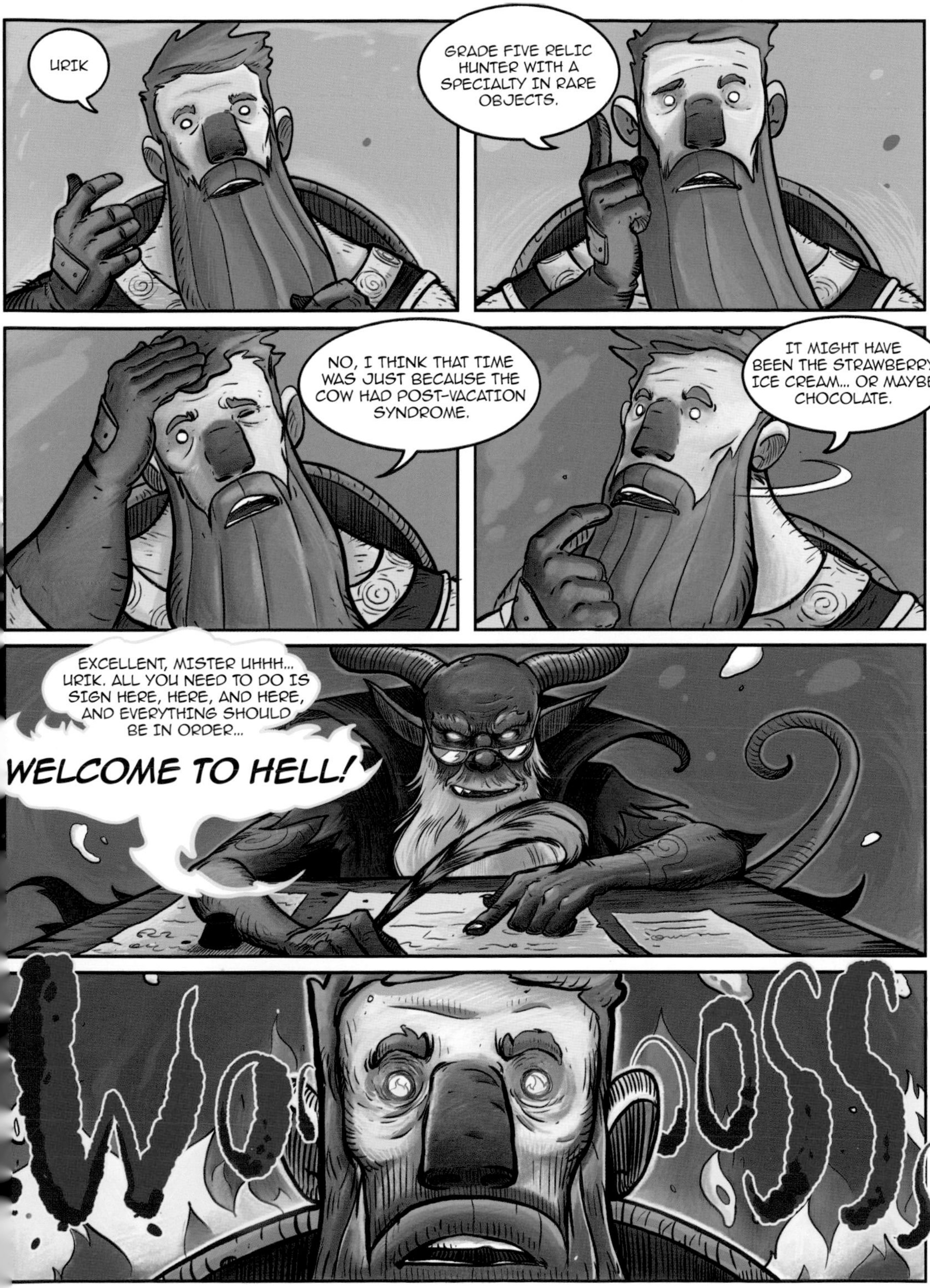
URIK
GRADE FIVE RELIC HUNTER WITH A SPECIALTY IN RARE OBJECTS.
NO, I THINK THAT TIME WAS JUST BECAUSE THE COW HAD POST-VACATION SYNDROME.
IT MIGHT HAVE BEEN THE STRAWBERRY ICE CREAM... OR MAYBE CHOCOLATE.
EXCELLENT, MISTER UHHH... URIK. ALL YOU NEED TO DO IS SIGN HERE, HERE, AND HERE, AND EVERYTHING SHOULD BE IN ORDER...
WELCOME TO HELL!
WOOSS

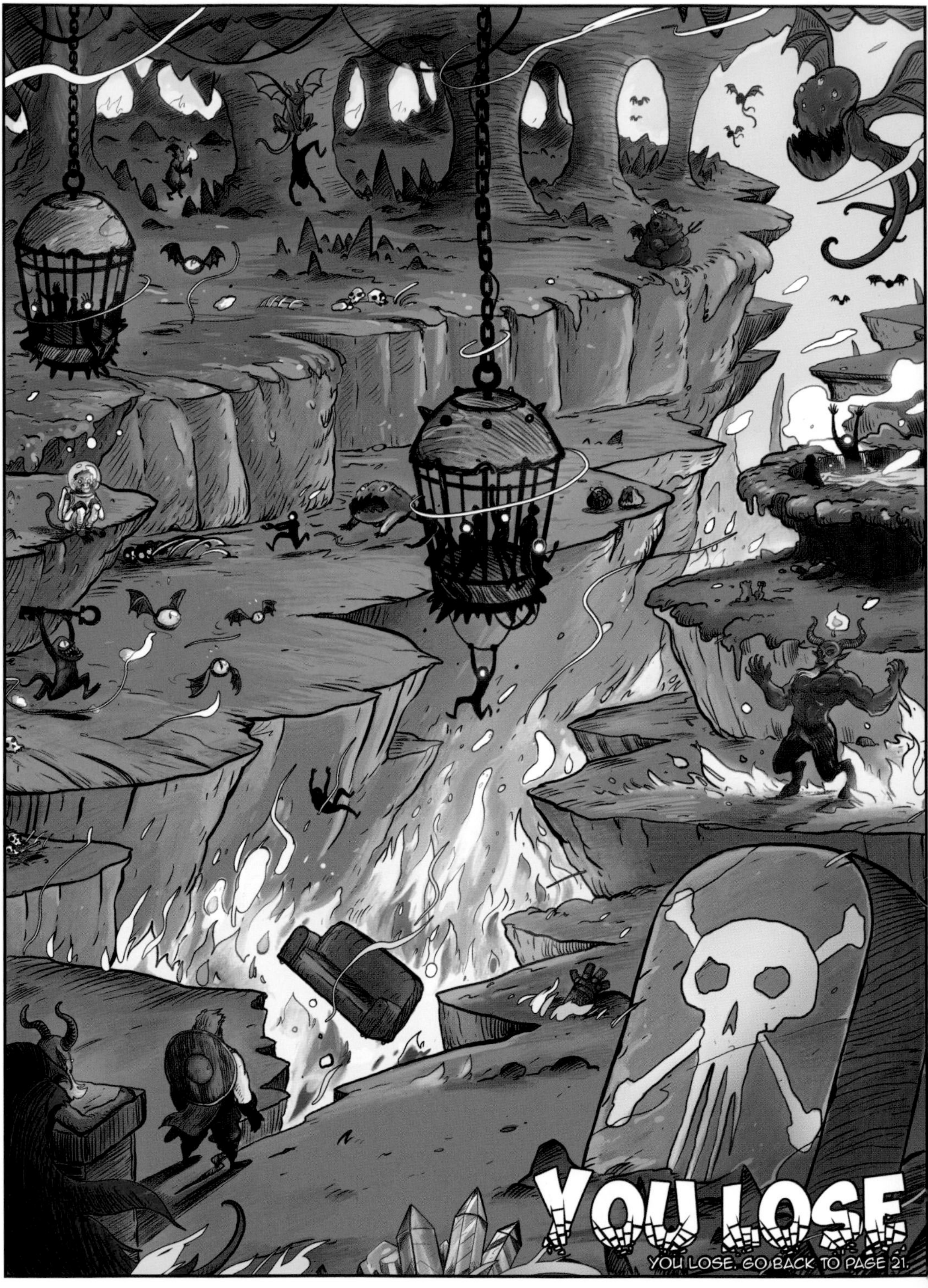
YOU LOSE
YOU LOSE. GO BACK TO PAGE 21.

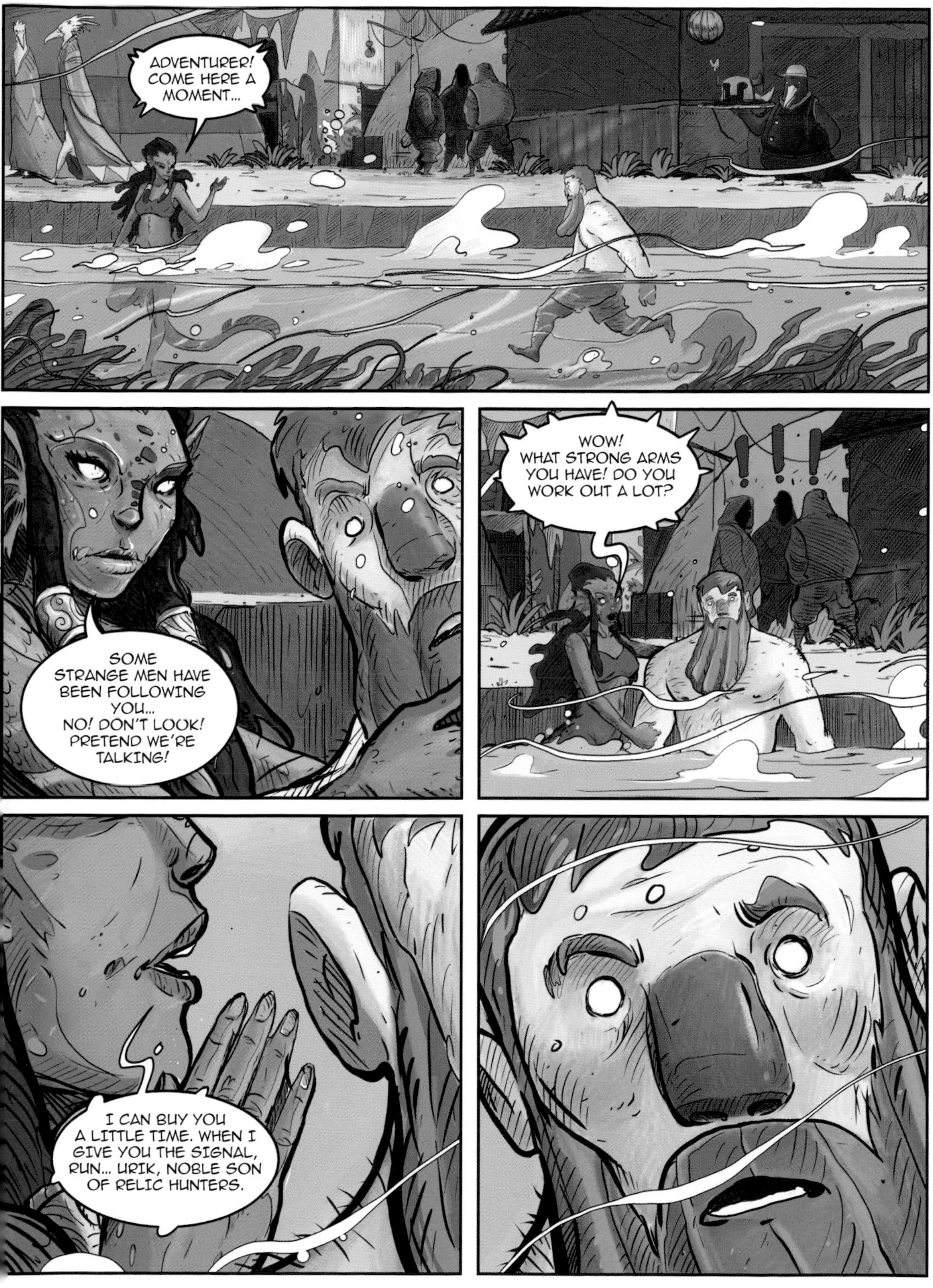
ADVENTURER! COME HERE A MOMENT...
SOME STRANGE MEN HAVE BEEN FOLLOWING YOU... NO! DON'T LOOK! PRETEND WE'RE TALKING!
WOW! WHAT STRONG ARMS YOU HAVE! DO YOU WORK OUT A LOT?
!!!
I CAN BUY YOU A LITTLE TIME. WHEN I GIVE YOU THE SIGNAL, RUN... URIK, NOBLE SON OF RELIC HUNTERS.

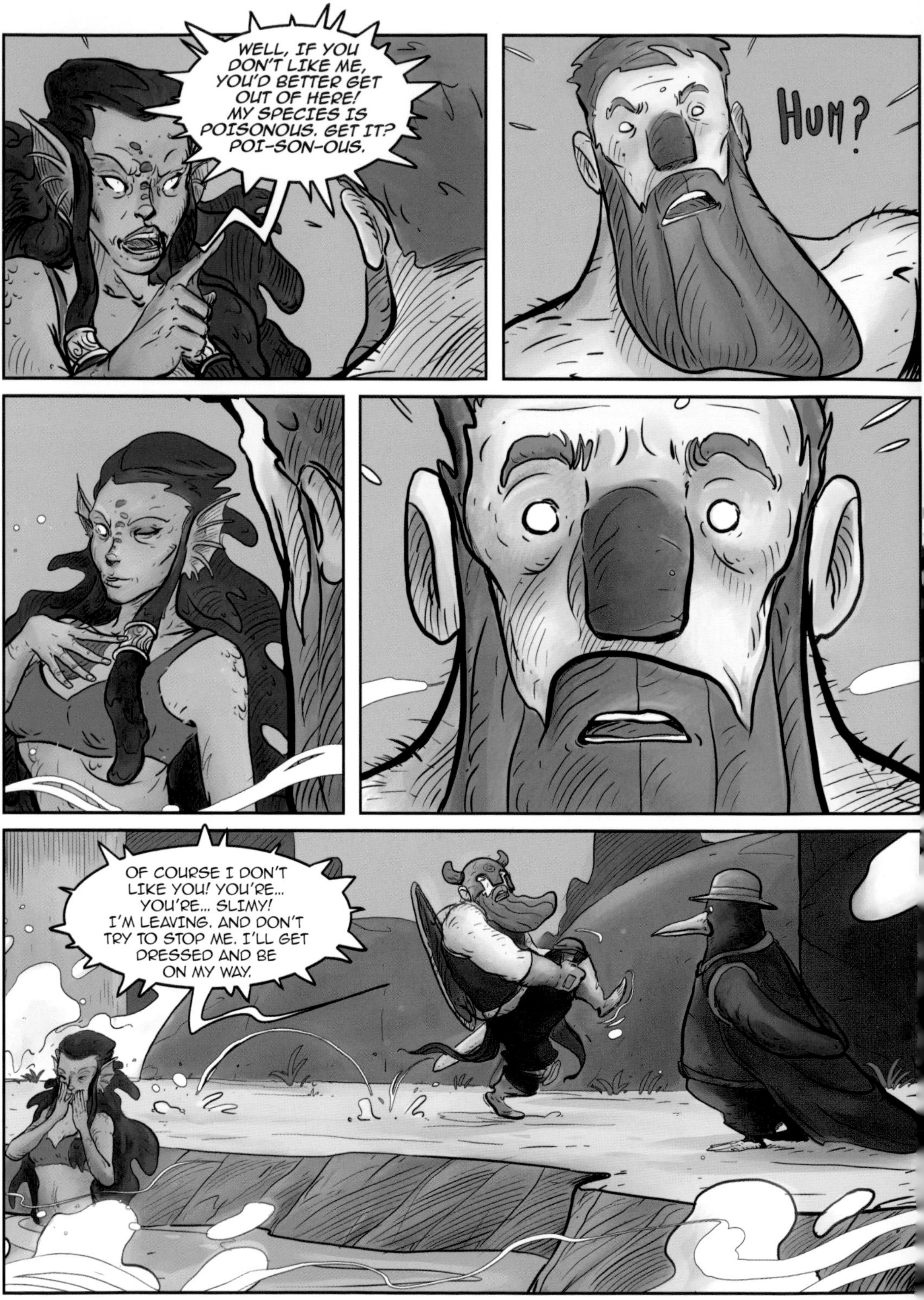
WELL, IF YOU DON'T LIKE ME, YOU'D BETTER GET OUT OF HERE! MY SPECIES IS POISONOUS. GET IT? POI-SON-OUS.
HUM?
OF COURSE I DON'T LIKE YOU! YOU'RE... YOU'RE... SLIMY! I'M LEAVING. AND DON'T TRY TO STOP ME. I'LL GET DRESSED AND BE ON MY WAY.

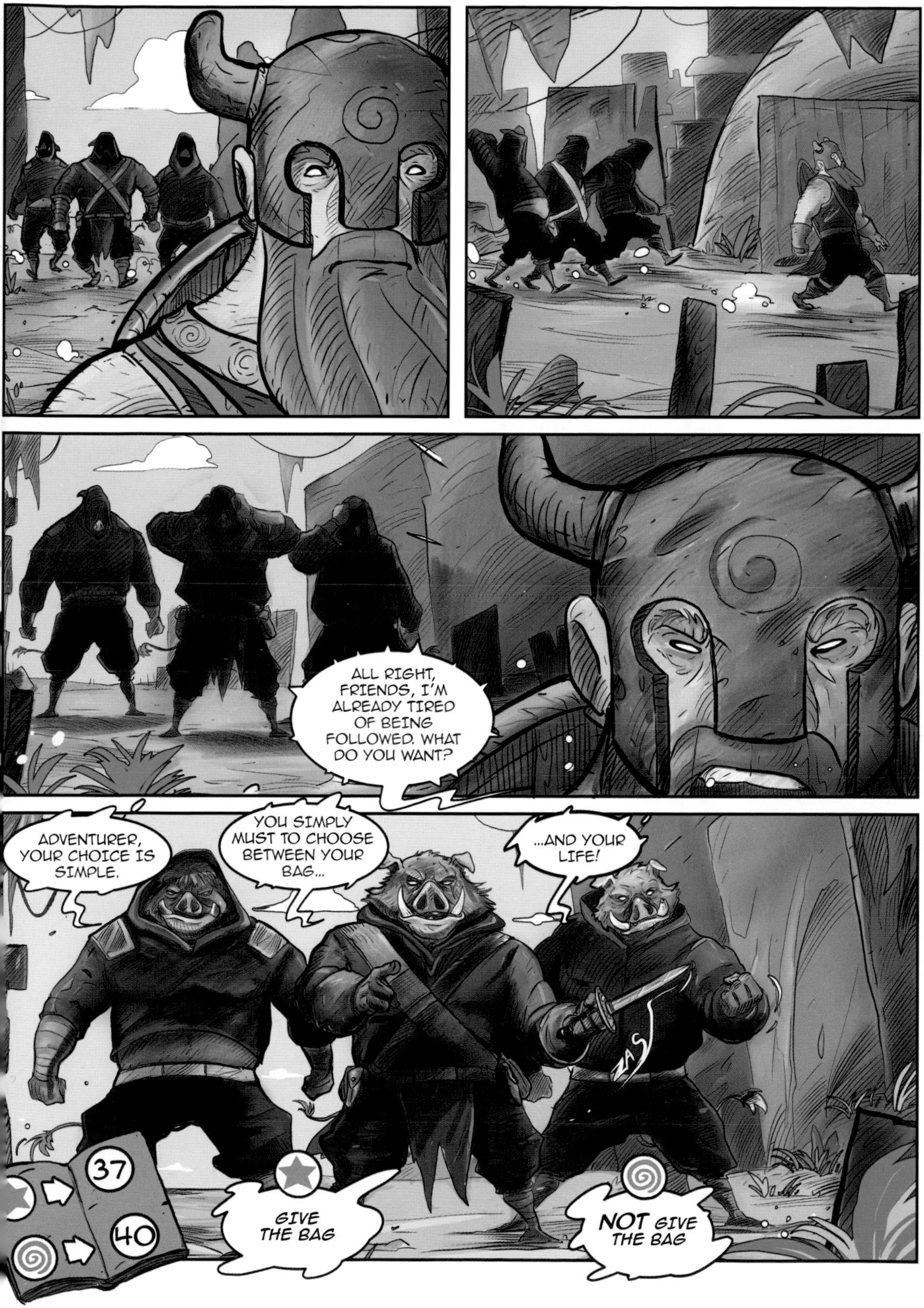
ALL RIGHT, FRIENDS, I'M ALREADY TIRED OF BEING FOLLOWED. WHAT DO YOU WANT?
ADVENTURER, YOUR CHOICE IS SIMPLE.
YOU SIMPLY MUST TO CHOOSE BETWEEN YOUR BAG...
...AND YOUR LIFE!
ZAS
37
40
GIVE THE BAG
NOT GIVE THE BAG

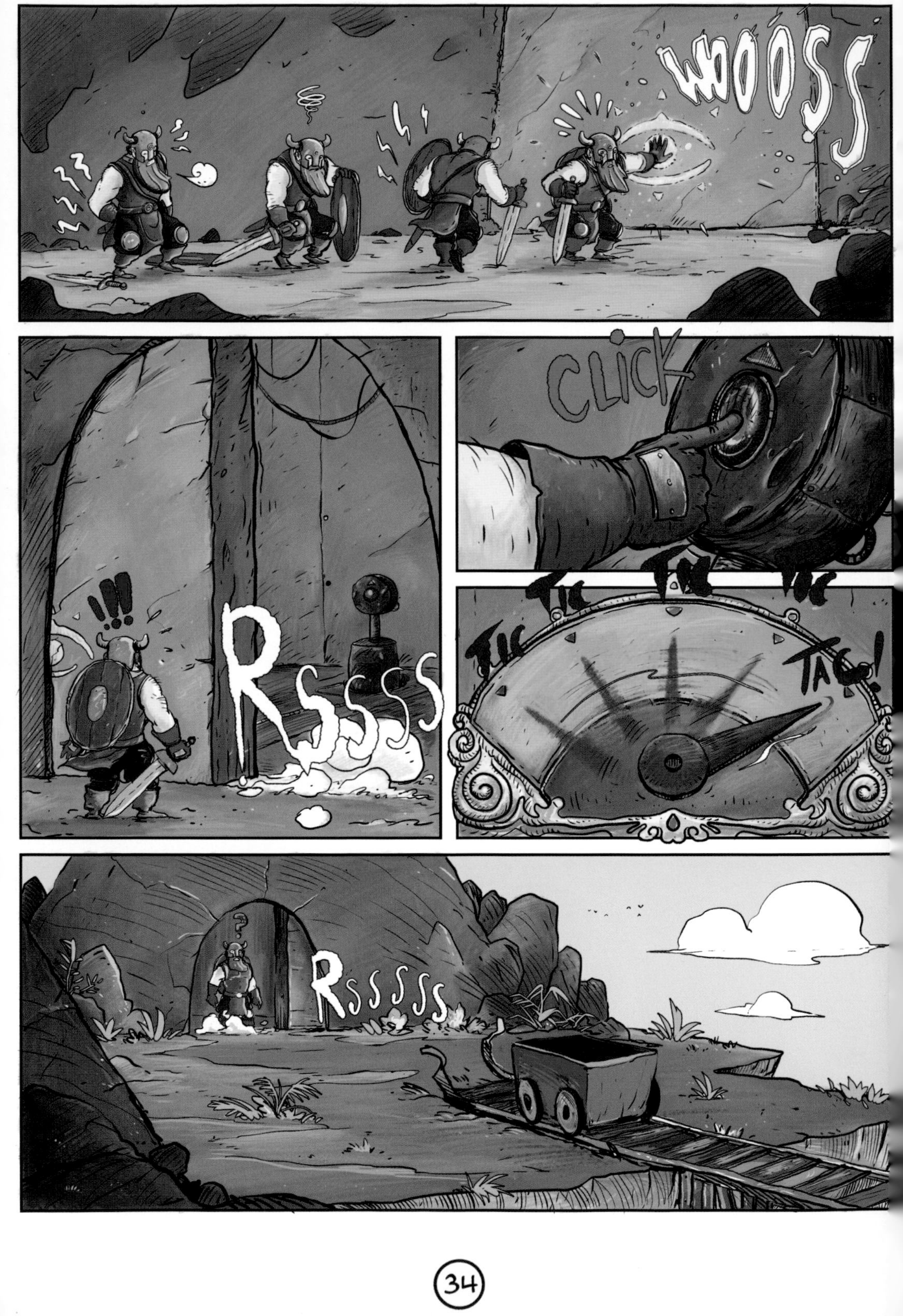
WOOSS
CLICK
RSSSSS
TIC
TIC
TAC!
RSSSSS

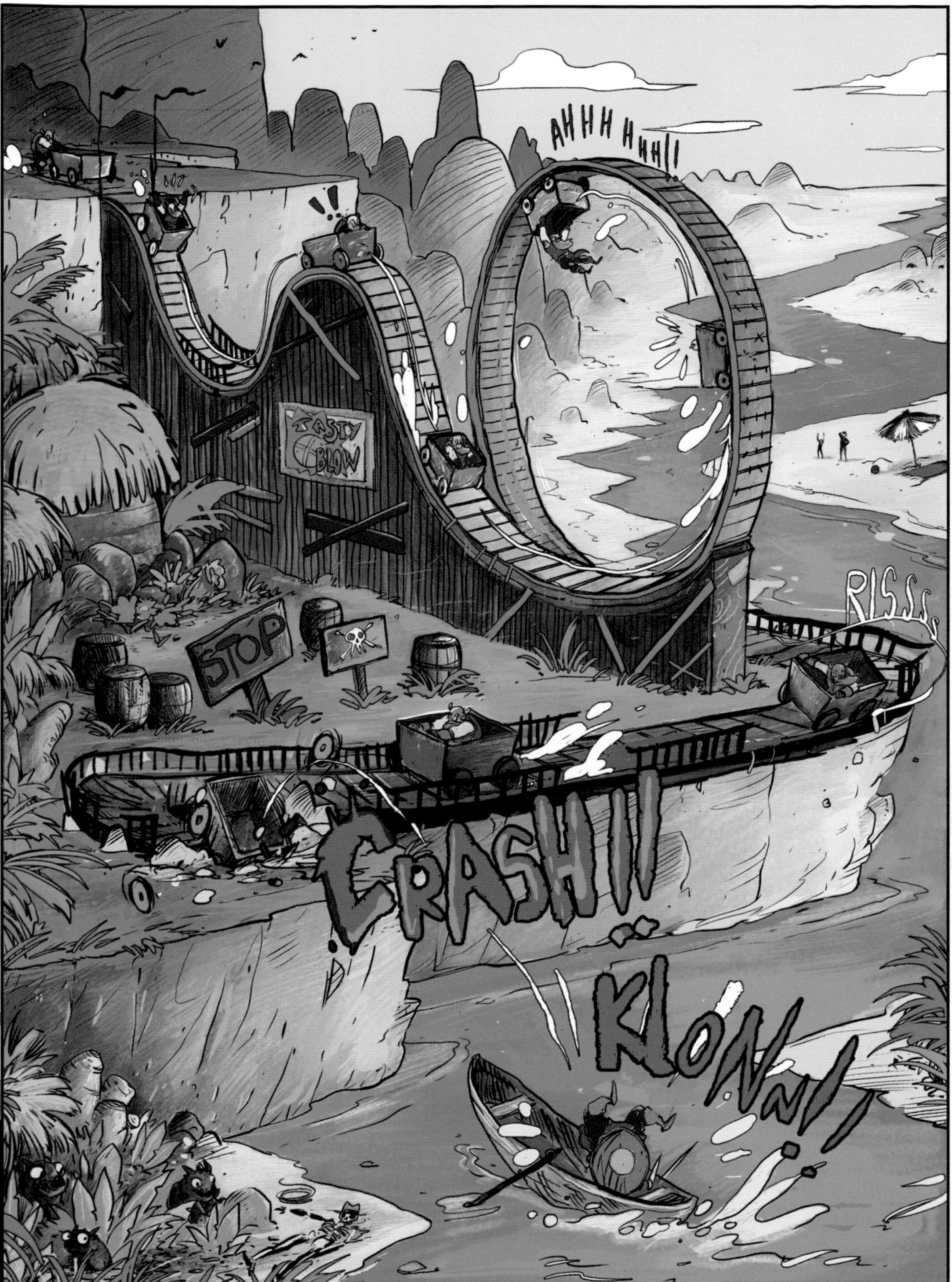
AHHHHHH!!
TASTY BLOW
STOP
RISSSs
CRASH!!
KLONNN!!

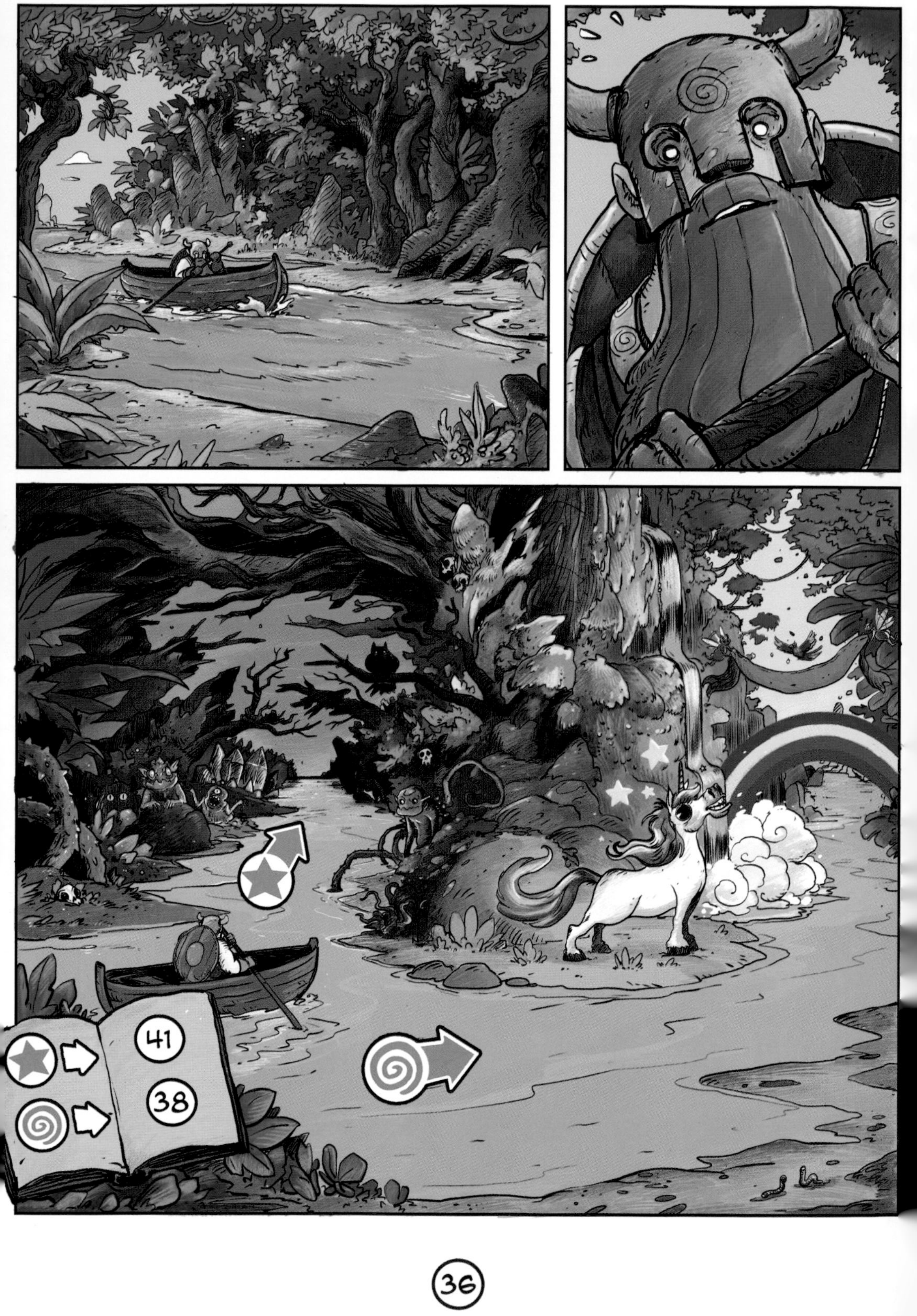
41
38

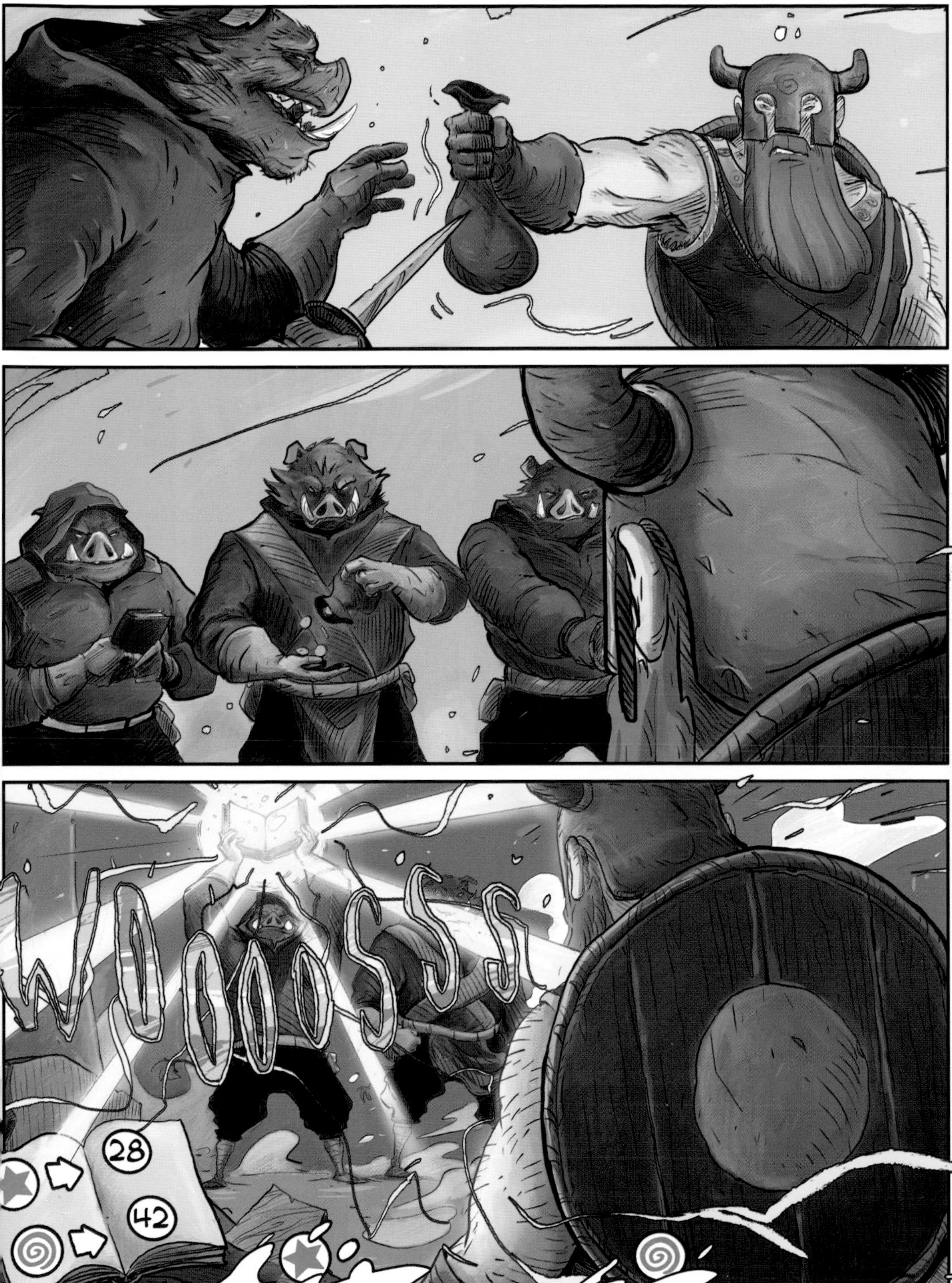
WOOOOSSS
28
42
STAY TO WATCH
FLEE

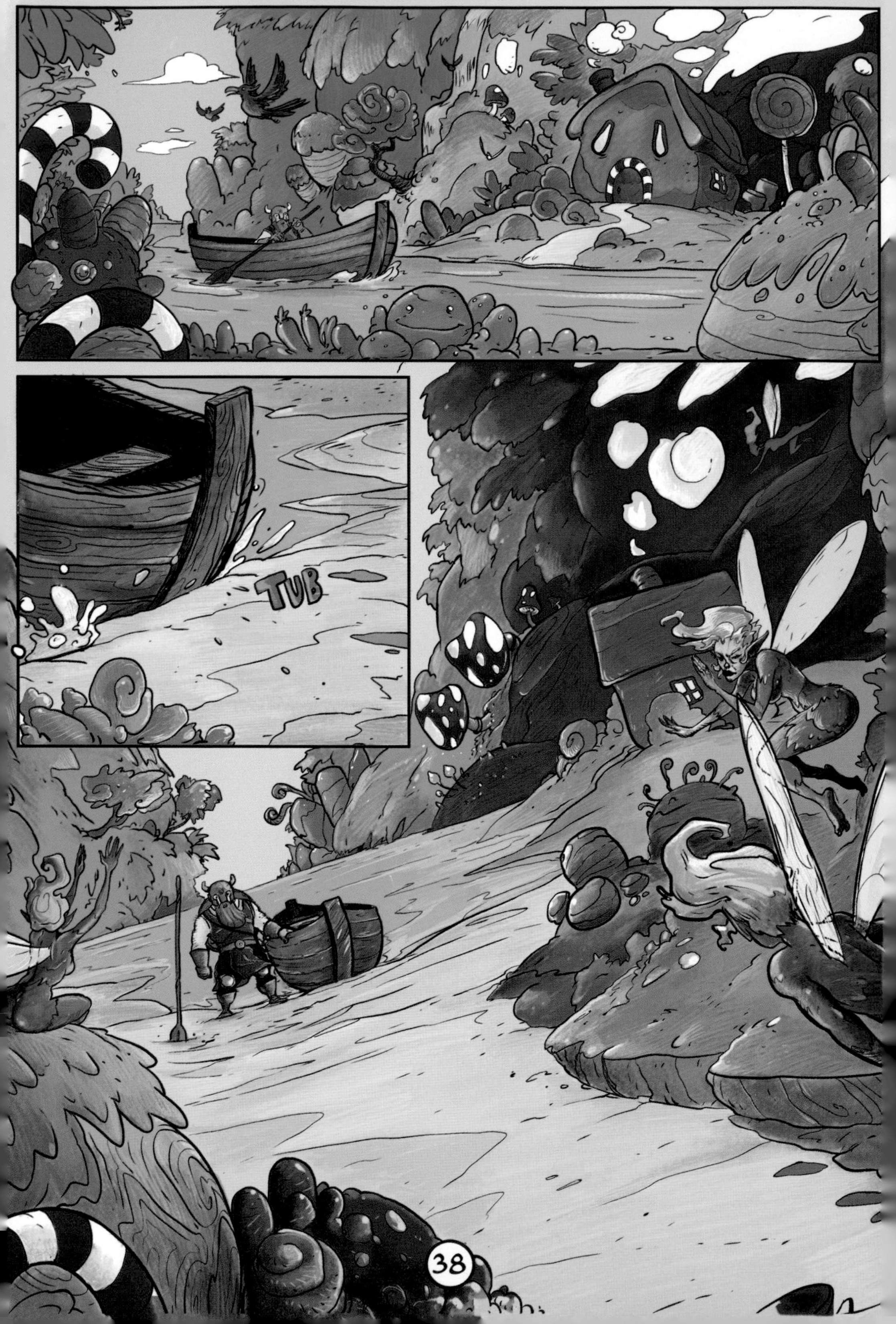
TUB

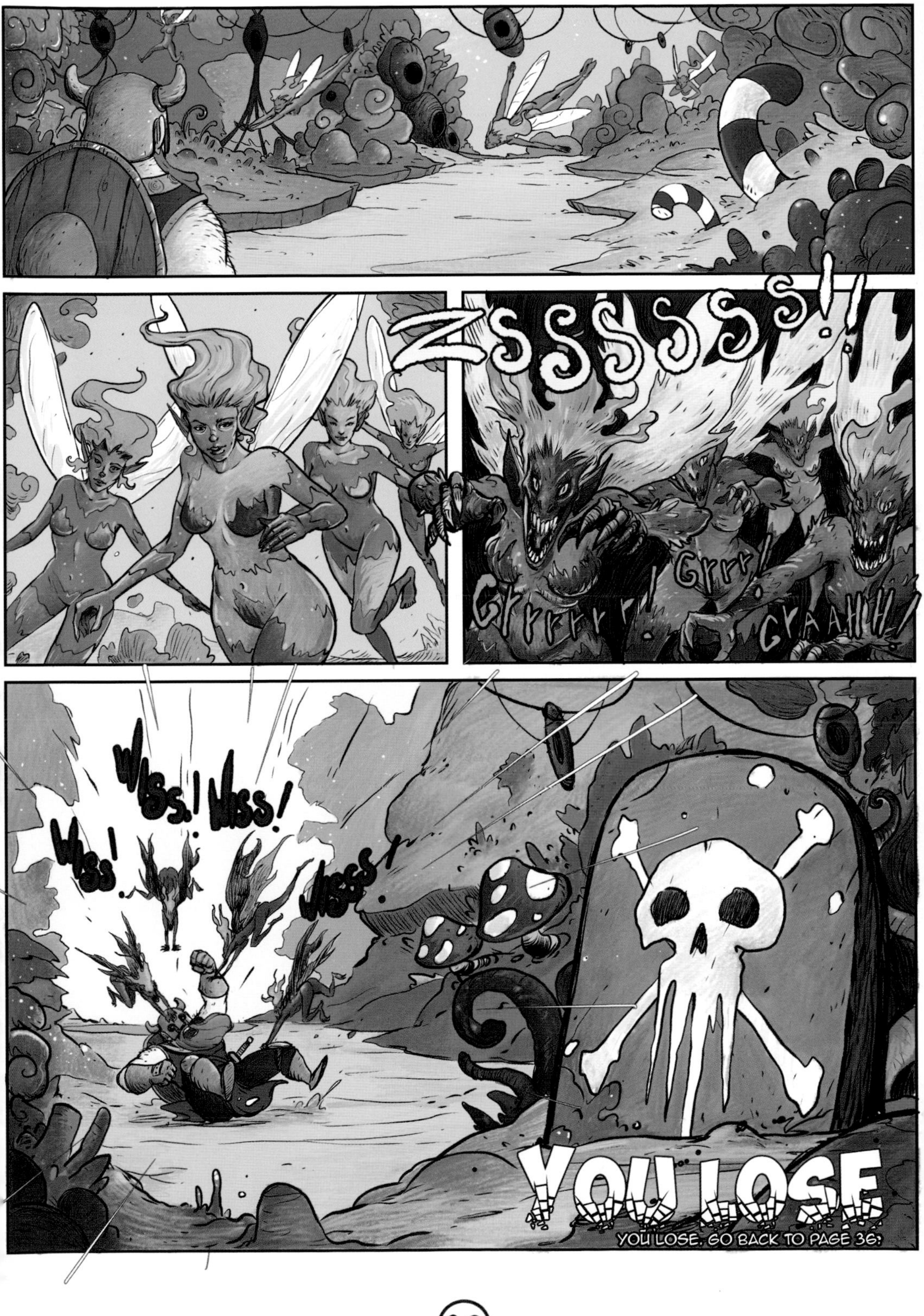
ZSSSSSSS!!
Grrrrrr!
Grrr!
GRAAHH!
WISS!
WISS!
WISS!
WISSS!
YOU LOSE
YOU LOSE. GO BACK TO PAGE 36.

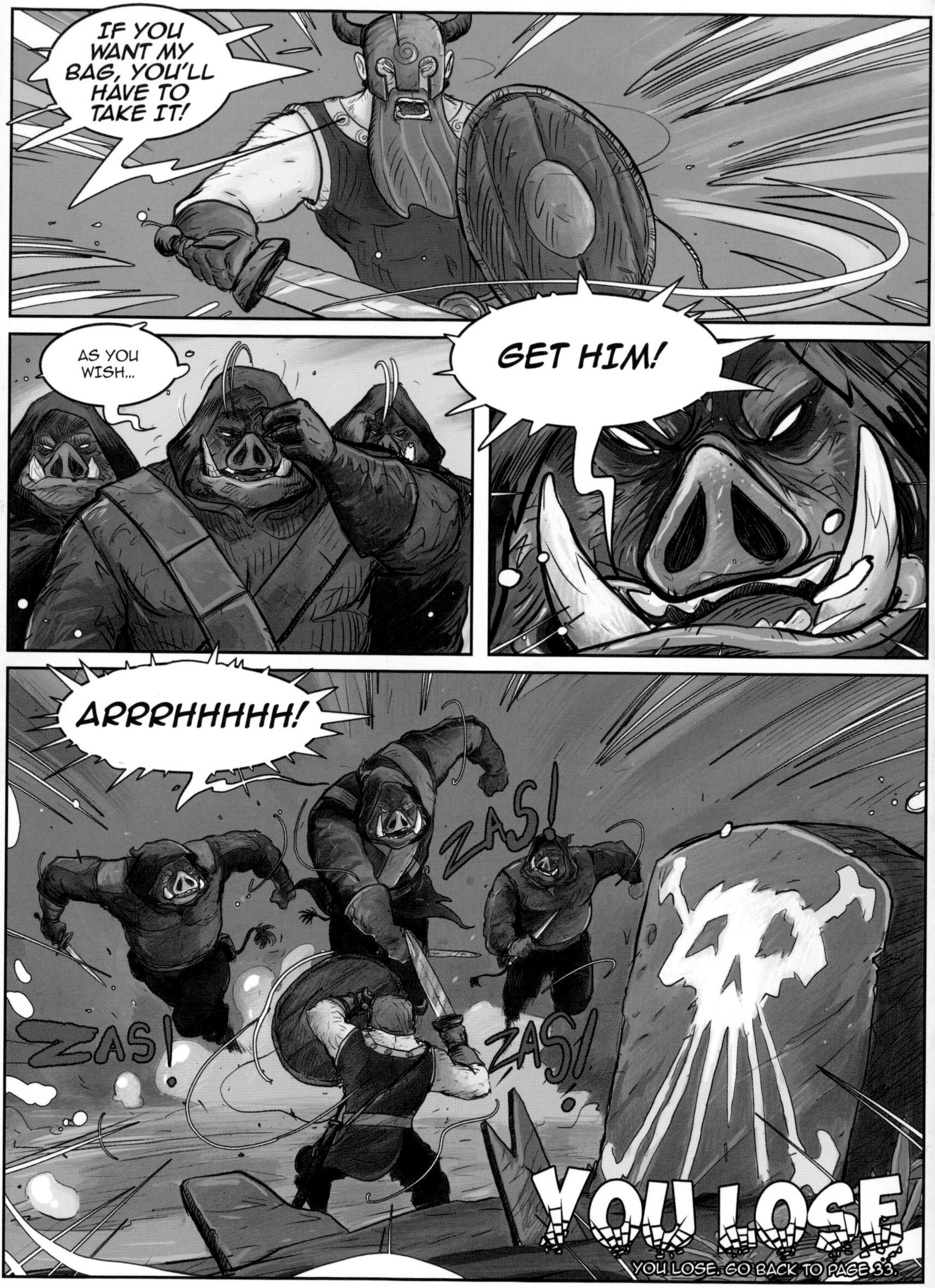
IF YOU WANT MY BAG, YOU'LL HAVE TO TAKE IT!
AS YOU WISH...
GET HIM!
ARRRHHHHH!
ZAS!
ZAS!
ZAS!
YOU LOSE
YOU LOSE. GO BACK TO PAGE 33.

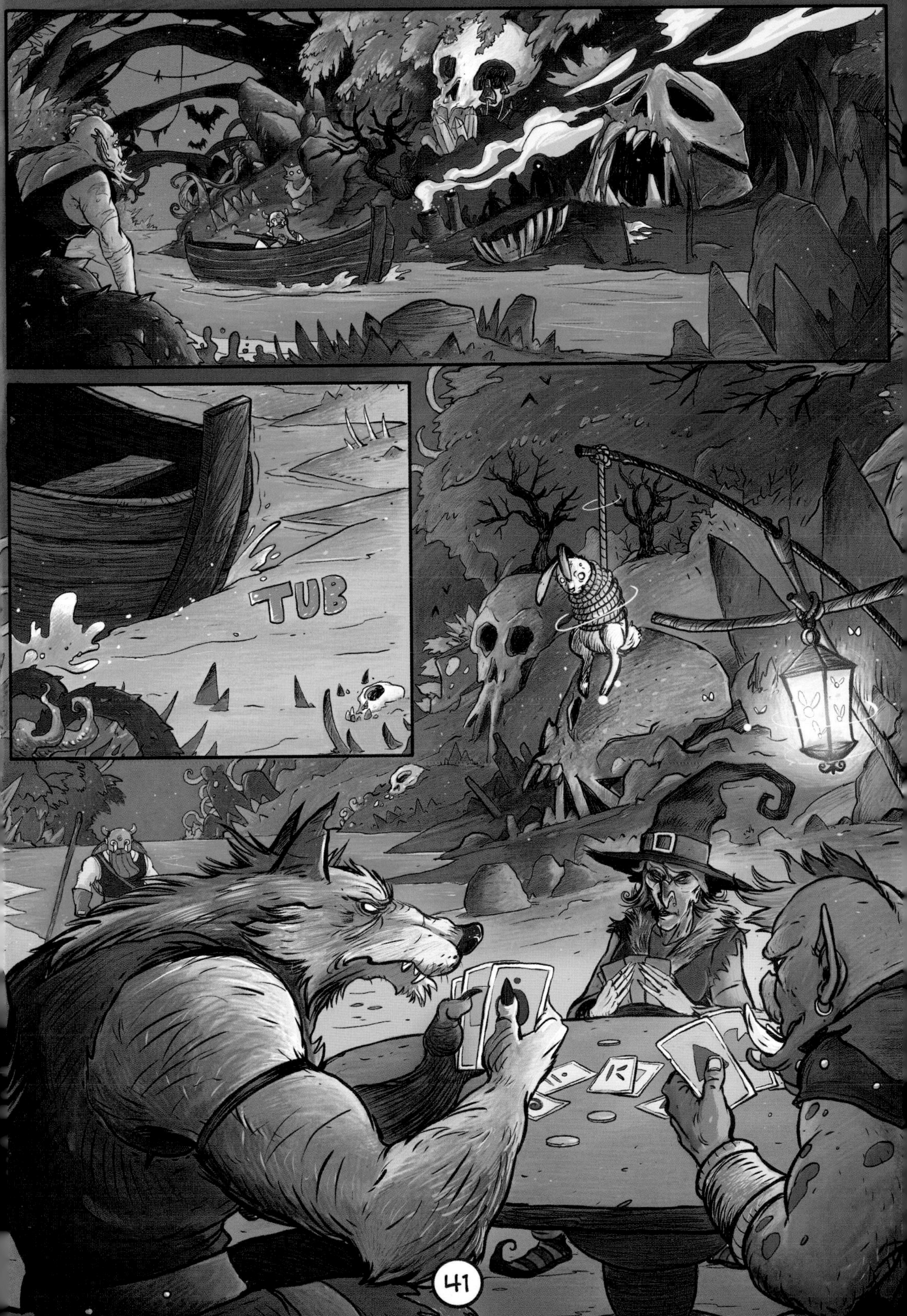
TUB

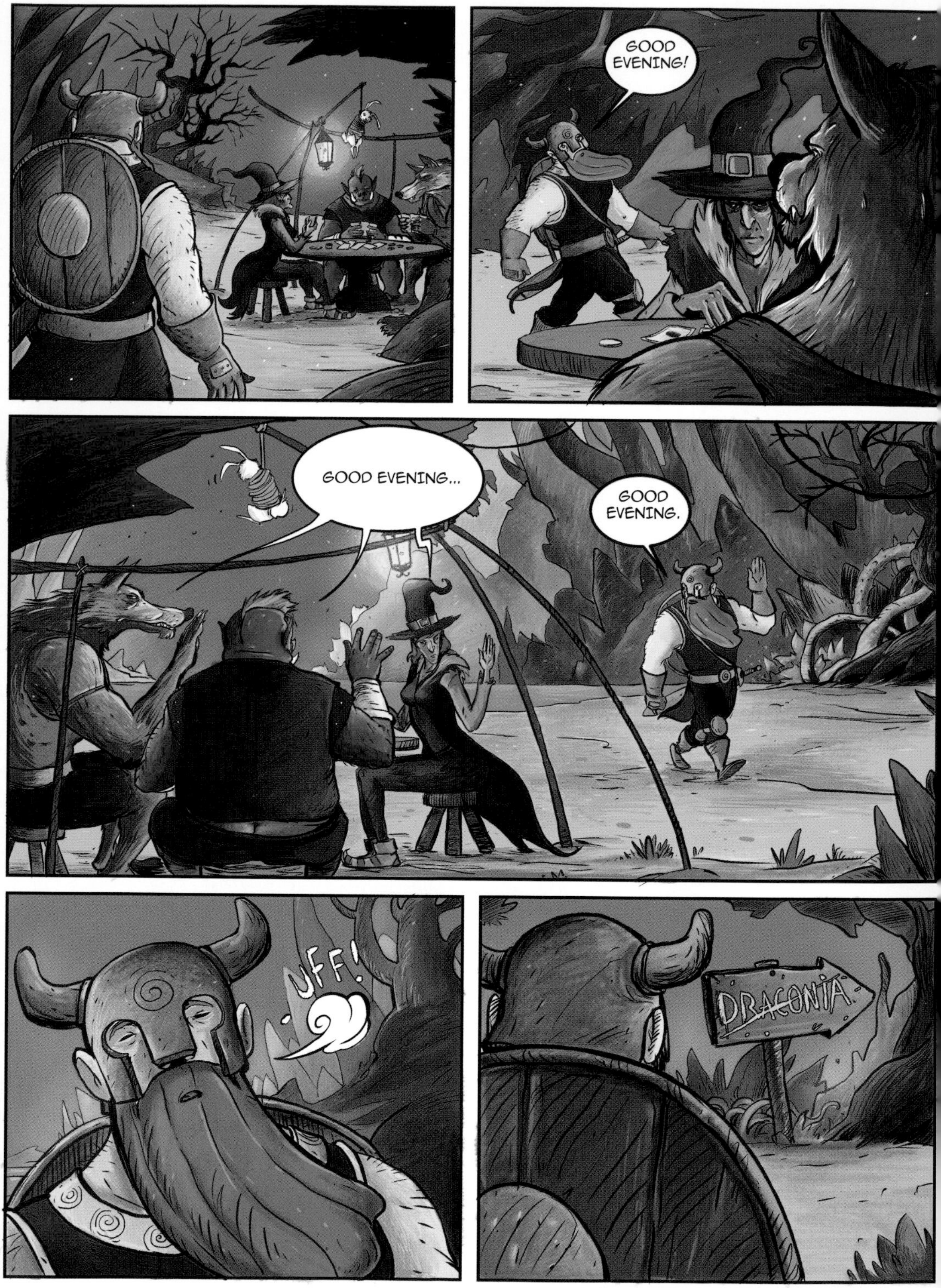
GOOD EVENING!
GOOD EVENING...
GOOD EVENING.
UFF!
DRACONIA

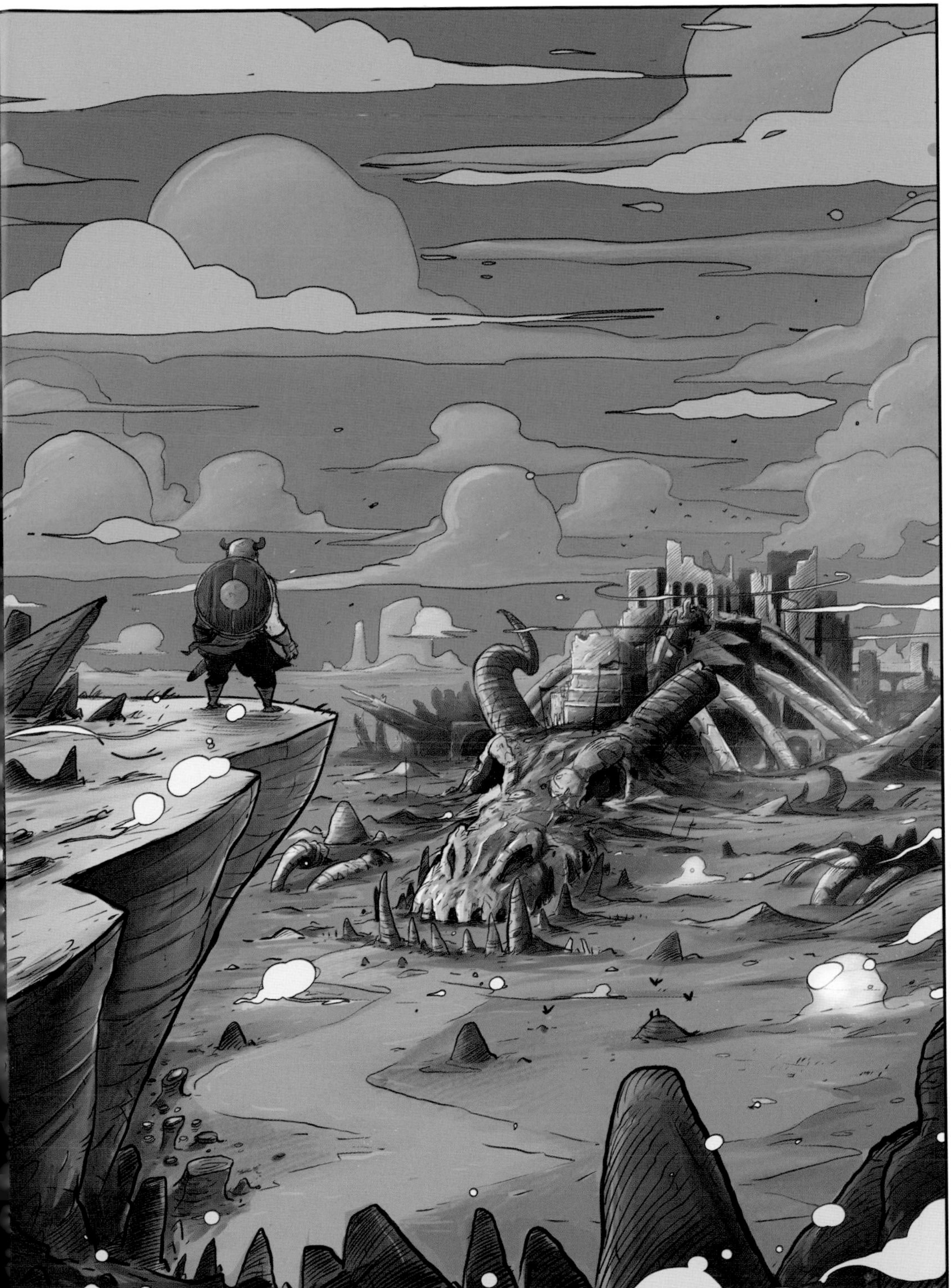

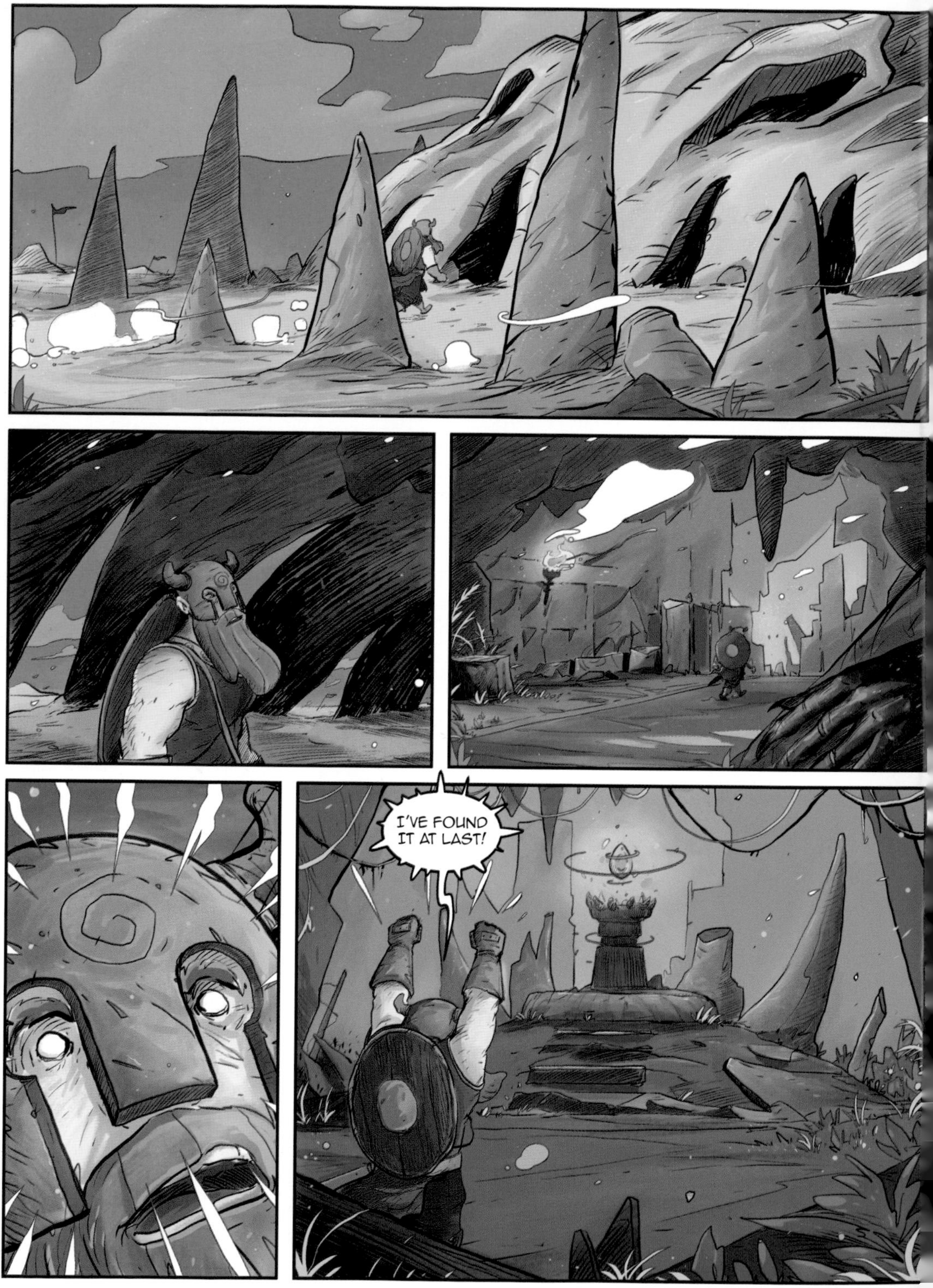
I'VE FOUND IT AT LAST!

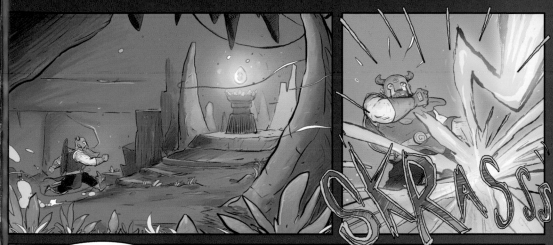

SKRASSS

HALT, FOOL!

WELL, WELL, WELL, TRAVELER...

YOU HAVE REACHED THE RUINED CITY OF DRACONIA. CONGRATULATIONS! BUT LIKE EVERY GREAT HERO WHO CAME BEFORE, YOU ARE NOW FACED WITH A DIFFICULT DECISION.

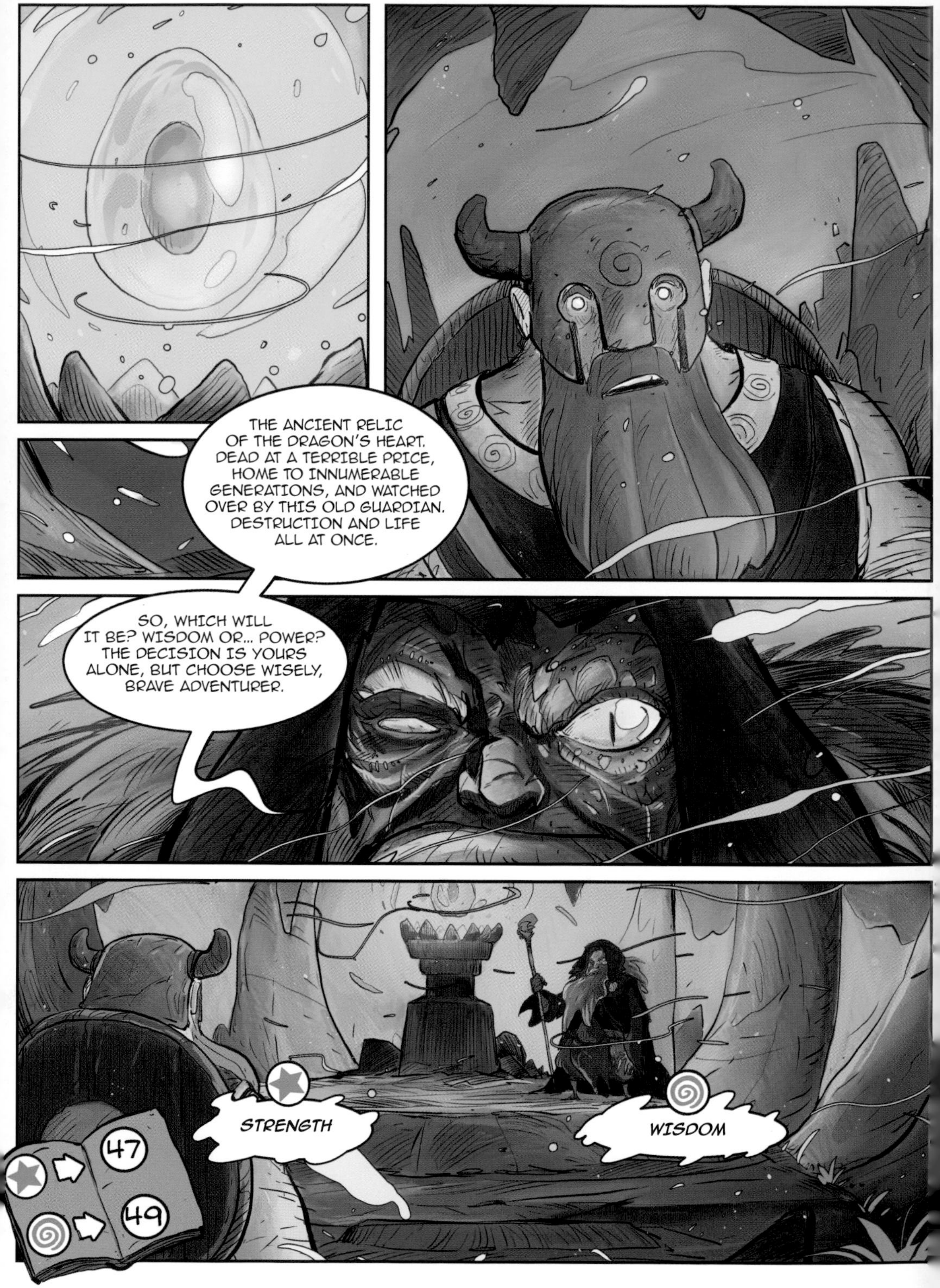
THE ANCIENT RELIC OF THE DRAGON'S HEART. DEAD AT A TERRIBLE PRICE, HOME TO INNUMERABLE GENERATIONS, AND WATCHED OVER BY THIS OLD GUARDIAN. DESTRUCTION AND LIFE ALL AT ONCE.
SO, WHICH WILL IT BE? WISDOM OR... POWER? THE DECISION IS YOURS ALONE, BUT CHOOSE WISELY, BRAVE ADVENTURER.
STRENGTH
WISDOM
47
49

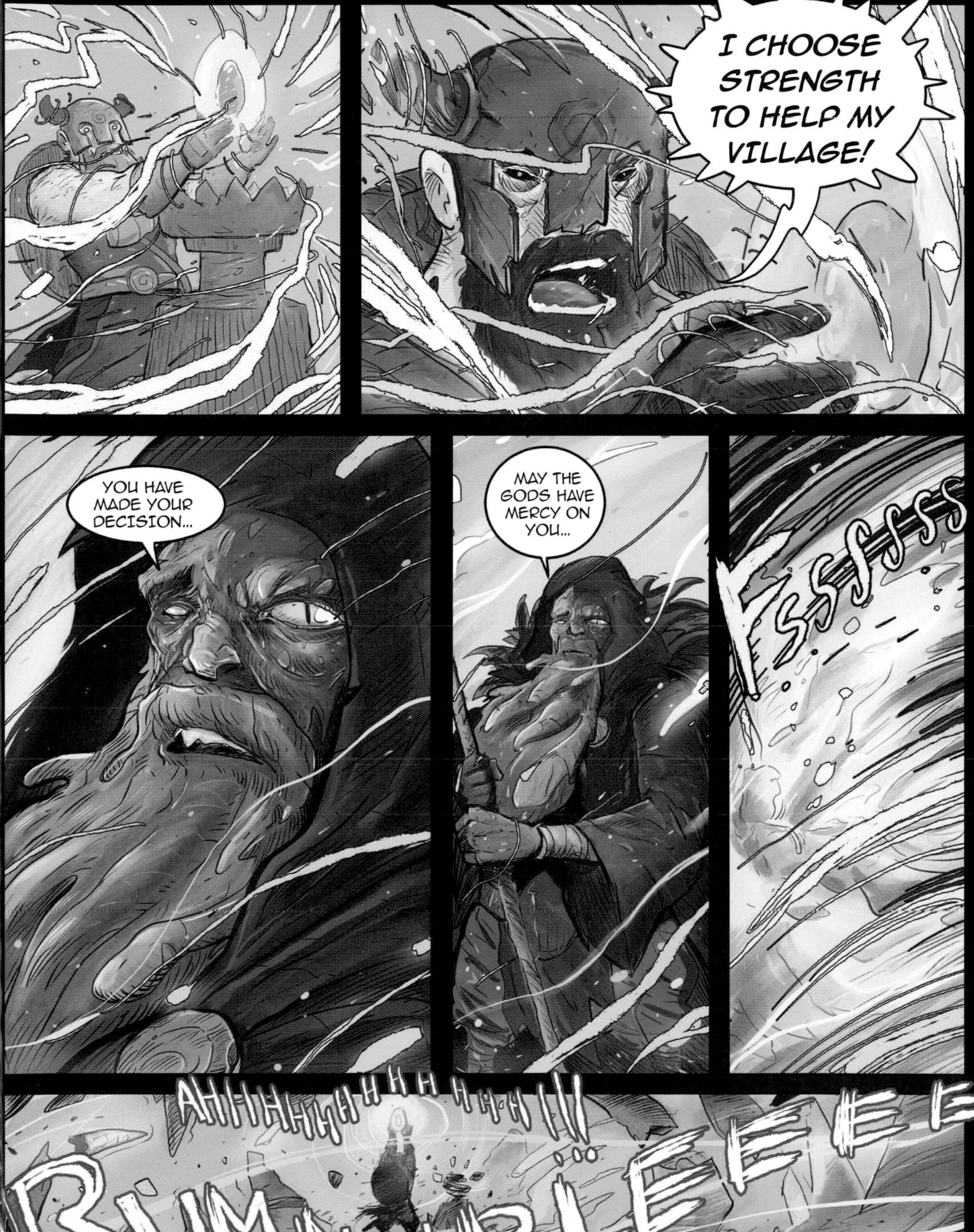
I CHOOSE STRENGTH TO HELP MY VILLAGE!
YOU HAVE MADE YOUR DECISION...
MAY THE GODS HAVE MERCY ON YOU...
FSSSSSSSS
AHHHHHHHHHHHHHH!!
RUMMMBLEEEEE

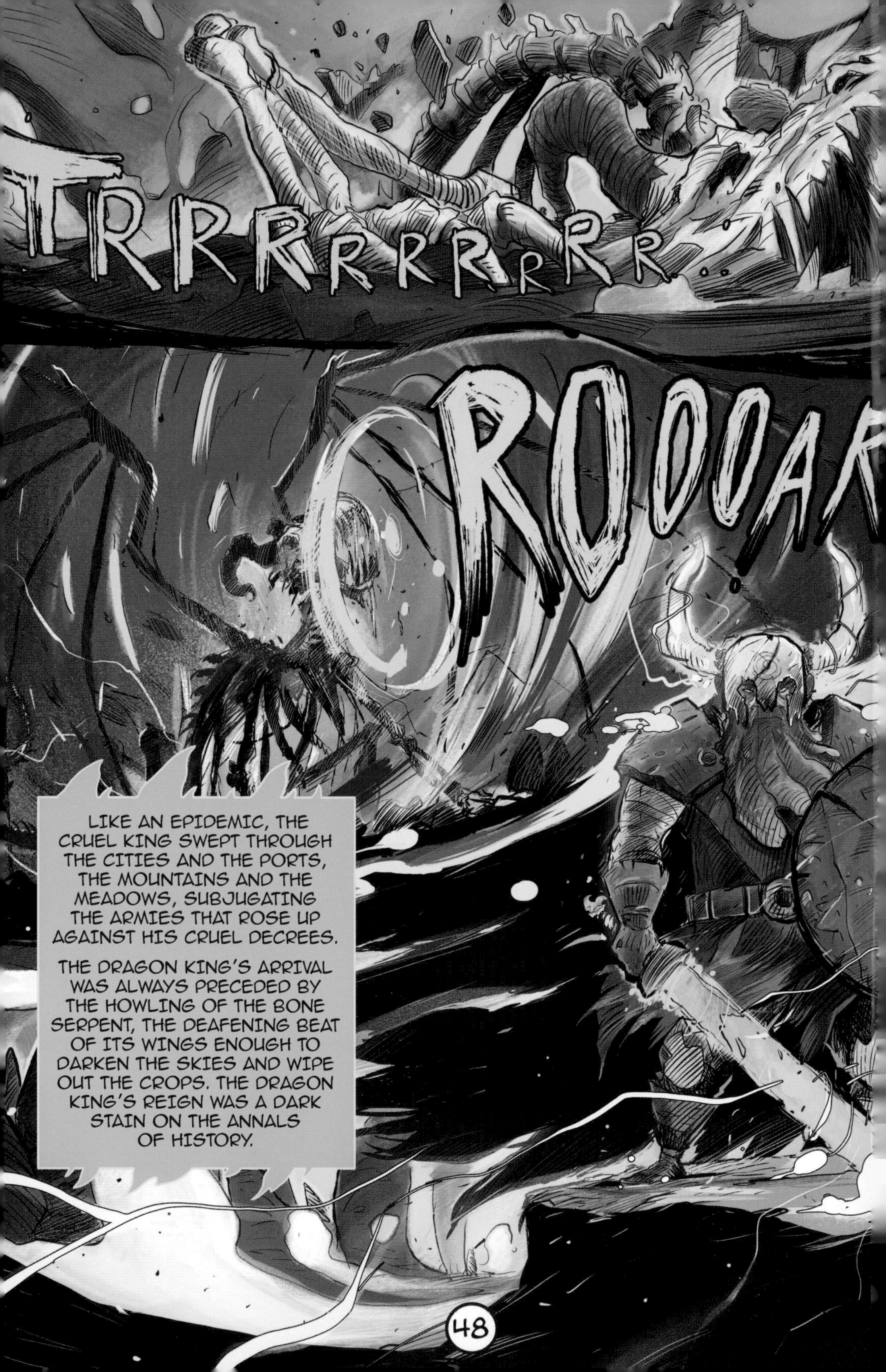
TRRRRRRRRR
ROOOAR
LIKE AN EPIDEMIC, THE CRUEL KING SWEPT THROUGH THE CITIES AND THE PORTS, THE MOUNTAINS AND THE MEADOWS, SUBJUGATING THE ARMIES THAT ROSE UP AGAINST HIS CRUEL DECREES.
THE DRAGON KING'S ARRIVAL WAS ALWAYS PRECEDED BY THE HOWLING OF THE BONE SERPENT, THE DEAFENING BEAT OF ITS WINGS ENOUGH TO DARKEN THE SKIES AND WIPE OUT THE CROPS. THE DRAGON KING'S REIGN WAS A DARK STAIN ON THE ANNALS OF HISTORY.

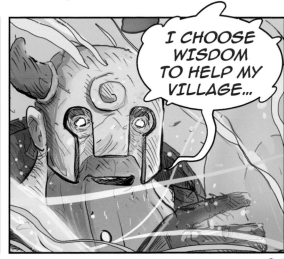

I CHOOSE WISDOM TO HELP MY VILLAGE...

EXCELLENT DECISION... GOOD LUCK, MY FRIEND.

FSSSS

SHUOOOAAA!!

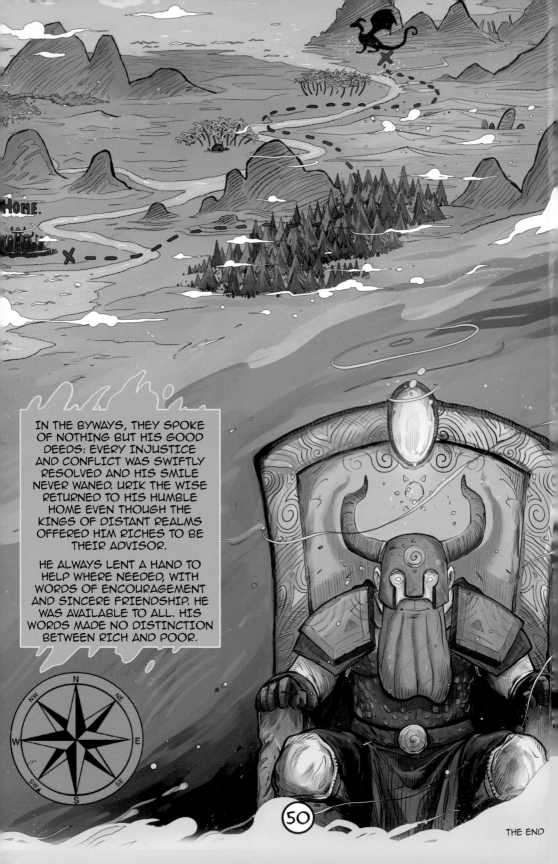

IN THE BYWAYS, THEY SPOKE OF NOTHING BUT HIS GOOD DEEDS: EVERY INJUSTICE AND CONFLICT WAS SWIFTLY RESOLVED AND HIS SMILE NEVER WANED. URIK THE WISE RETURNED TO HIS HUMBLE HOME EVEN THOUGH THE KINGS OF DISTANT REALMS OFFERED HIM RICHES TO BE THEIR ADVISOR.

HE ALWAYS LENT A HAND TO HELP WHERE NEEDED, WITH WORDS OF ENCOURAGEMENT AND SINCERE FRIENDSHIP. HE WAS AVAILABLE TO ALL. HIS WORDS MADE NO DISTINCTION BETWEEN RICH AND POOR.

HOME.

50

THE END

RELIC OF THE DRAGON
CREATOR BIOS

MIGUEL ÁNGEL GARCÍA

MIGUEL ÁNGEL GARCÍA WAS BORN ON SEPTEMBER 27, 1984. SINCE HIS CHILDHOOD, HE'S FOCUSED HIS LIFE ON ART AND ILLUSTRATION. *RELIC OF THE DRAGON* IS HIS FIRST BOOK PUBLISHED IN THE UNITED STATES, INSPIRED BY THE CHOOSE-YOUR-OWN ADVENTURE BOOKS OF THE 1990s AND THE DESIRE TO INTERTWINE THE PROTAGONIST'S AND READER'S FATES!

ADRIAN BENATAR

BORN IN A SMALL TOWN NEAR THE CHANNEL WHOSE NAME HE DOES NOT WANT TO REMEMBER, ADRIAN BEGAN TO WRITE ALMOST BEFORE HE BEGAN TO SPEAK. LONG INTERESTED IN SCIENCE, THOUGH MATHEMATICS HAS FOREVER BEEN AN ARCHENEMY, ADRIAN WILL TRY TO WRITE ANYTHING ONCE EVEN TRYING TO REPAIR A LEAK BY TYPING! (IT DIDN'T WORK.) HE CURRENTLY LIVES WITH HIS FAMILY, A BLACK CAT, A BLACK DOG, AND HIS BLACK BEARD. HE HOPES TO CONTINUE WRITING THROUGHOUT HIS LIFE.

SPECIAL THANKS

THANKS TO TED ADAMS AND IDW PUBLISHING FOR BELIEVING IN MY WORK. THANKS TO MY FAMILY FOR THE SUPPORT AND THE TOOLS THAT HAVE CARRIED ME THROUGHOUT MY LIFE, WITHOUT THEM THIS WOULD NEVER HAVE BEEN POSSIBLE. THANKS TO MY PARTNER ANA –AN IMPORTANT PILLAR IN MY LIFE THAT SUPPORTS ME DAY BY DAY. AND THANKS TO ADRIAN FOR WANTING TO WORK WITH ME. THANKS TO ALL OF YOU.

~MIGUEL

TO THE ENTIRE IDW TEAM FOR ALL THE WORK DONE AND TO TED ADAMS FOR TRUSTING US. TO SANDRA CAÑADAS FOR PUSHING ME TO DARE AND TO KEEP TRYING. TO MY FAMILY FOR TAKING CARE OF ME AS WELL AS THEY HAVE. TO MIGUEL ÁNGEL FOR MAKING THE DIFFICULT, EASY... AND VICE VERSA. THANKS TO ALL THOSE PEOPLE WHO NEVER TRUSTED ME AND THOSE WHO SET BARRIERS AND OBSTACLES FOR ME... YOU ONLY MADE ME STRONGER. AND FINALLY, TO YOU... THE PERSON WHO READS THIS COMIC, I HOPE YOU LIKE IT.

~ADRIAN

Relic of the Dragon

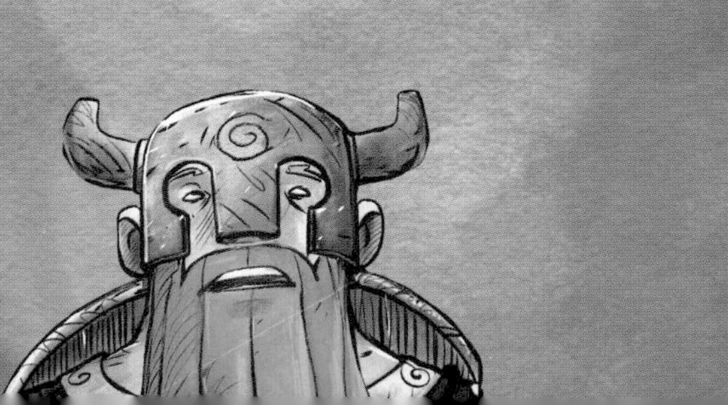